"TAKE IT!" she hissed. "Wear it. Learn what it is to be what I am."

Rowan hesitated. The last thing in the world he wanted to do was to obey. But his hand stretched out without his willing it, and before he could think the medallion was glowing warm between his fingers, and he was slipping the cord around his own neck. The medallion was heavy—far heavier than he remembered. It seemed to weigh him down.

Sheba slumped back into her chair, as if with relief.

"So—it is done," she muttered. "Go now."

**READ ABOUT
ALL OF ROWAN'S ADVENTURES
IN THE ROWAN OF RIN SERIES:**

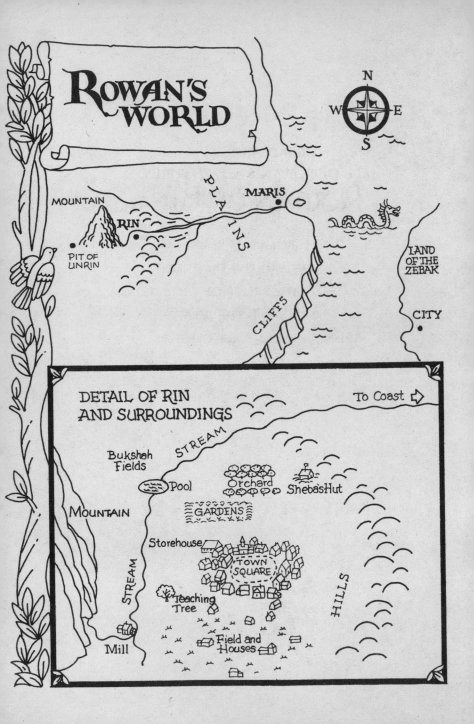

EMILY RODDA

Rowan
and the
Ice Creepers

A Greenwillow Book

Avon Books
An Imprint of HarperCollins*Publishers*

First published in Australia in 2003 by Omnibus Books, an imprint of Scholastic
Australia Pty Ltd. under the title *Rowan of the Bukshah*
First published in the United States in 2003 by Greenwillow Books, an imprint of
HarperCollins Publishers, by arrangement with Scholastic Australia Pty Ltd.

Library of Congress Cataloging-in-Publication Data
Rodda, Emily.
Rowan and the Ice Creepers / by Emily Rodda.
p. cm.
"Greenwillow Books."
Summary: When a bitter winter threatens starvation to the people of Rin who set out
for the coast, Rowan and several others stay behind for various reasons and are led to a
startling discovery about their people's past.
ISBN 0-06-029780-8 — ISBN 0-06-029781-6 (lib. bdg.)
ISBN 0-06-441023-4 (pbk.)
[1. Heroes—Fiction.   2. Fantasy.]   I. Title.   PZ7.R5996Ri 2003   [Fic]—
dc21   2003000154

First Avon edition, 2004

AVON TRADEMARK REG. U.S. PAT. OFF. AND IN OTHER COUNTRIES,
MARCA REGISTRADA, HECHO EN U.S.A.

❖

Visit us on the World Wide Web!
www.harperchildrens.com

To my family
who asked for more about Rowan

CONTENTS

1 ∾ "It Is a Curse!"

 The village of Rin huddled, freezing, in a silent world of white. Deep snow blanketed the valley. The Mountain brooded against the gray sky like a vast ice sculpture capped with cloud.

Never had there been a winter like this. Never had the snow fallen so thickly. Never had the cold been so bitter.

And never had it lasted so long. By the calendar, it was spring—the time for planting, and for blossom, bees, and nesting birds. But still the air was deadly chill, fields and gardens lay buried, and snow weighed down the bare branches of the trees in Strong Jonn's orchard.

A meeting was called, but it was too cold for the people to gather in the village square. They crowded

instead in the House of Books, shivering and murmuring amid the smell of oil lamps, parchment, and
old paper. Deep shadows flickered on worried faces,
gesturing hands. The lamps were turned low, for oil,
like everything else, was in short supply.

Rowan, who had been in the bukshah field when
the meeting bell sounded, arrived last of all.

For a time he stood outside the door, stamping the
snow from his boots. Despite the cold, he was in no
hurry to enter. He knew what old Lann, the village
leader, was going to say to the people, and he had
made his own decision on what he was going to do
about it. For now, his mind was still with the bukshah.

The great gentle beasts he tended had strayed
again during the night. They tried it every winter,
but this year they had broken out of their field
over and over again.

This time they had wandered past the silent mill,
its huge wheel stuck fast in the ice of the stream,
and moved on till they had almost reached the
base of the Mountain. It had taken hours to tempt
them back to their field—hours, and the last few
handfuls of oats from the storehouse.

There will be trouble when it is discovered those
oats are gone, Rowan thought ruefully. But what
else could I do? Let the bukshah wander off to die?

He did not blame the beasts for breaking down their fence. They were hungry. The bales of hay on which they fed in winter were almost gone, and in a desperate attempt to make the food last, Rowan had been forced to cut their daily ration by half. Several of the oldest and frailest members of the herd had already weakened and died.

But Rowan knew that if food was scarce in the valley, it did not exist at all outside it. Except where sheer, rocky cliffs showed as brutal gashes on the shimmering whiteness of the Mountain, the land was snow covered on every side, as far as the eye could see.

"You must stop trying to stray, Star," Rowan had said to his favorite, the leader of the herd, when at last all the beasts were back in their field. "You must stay here where I can care for you."

Star had turned her great head to look at him and rumbled deep in her throat. Her small dark eyes were troubled. She wanted to please Rowan and obey him. But all her instincts were telling her that he was wrong.

Dimly understanding, Rowan had patted her, feeling with dismay the jutting ribs beneath her shaggy coat. "Spring will surely come soon, Star," he had whispered. "The snow will melt and there will be grass for you to eat once more. Just a little longer..."

But how *much* longer? Rowan thought now. How long can this go on?

Gritting his teeth, he pushed open the door and slipped into the crowded room. Shaaran and Norris, the two young people he had rescued from the enemy land of the Zebak, moved quickly to his side. They had clearly been watching for him. Shaaran's soft eyes were anxious, but her brother's face was alive with curiosity.

"Where have you been hiding yourself, Rowan?" Norris whispered. "We have not seen you for days!" He grinned and glanced at his sister teasingly. "Shaaran thinks you have been avoiding us. She fears we have done something to offend you. Please put her out of her misery and tell her it is not so."

"Norris!" Shaaran hissed, blushing scarlet.

Rowan forced a smile. "Of course you have not offended me," he murmured. That at least he could say truly, though he could not deny the rest. How could he have been with his friends and not told them what was about to happen? So he had avoided them.

But now they were about to hear everything. His heart ached at the thought of their dismay.

Norris would have pressed him further, but at that moment there was movement at the front of the room. Lann was preparing to speak. She was standing in the place of honor, in front of the hanging strips of painted silk that told in pictures the ancient story of the Rin people's slavery in the land of the Zebak. The bright paintings, glimmering in the lamplight, made a strange background to her sober figure.

For more than three hundred years the Rin people had lived in freedom in their green valley, with no memory of their past and no idea that many of their own had been left behind in the dreaded place across the sea. Then, just over a year before, Rowan's little sister Annad had been snatched away and carried to the land of the Zebak.

Determined to save her, Rowan had followed. He had found her, against all odds. And at the same time he had found Shaaran and Norris, the last of the lost ones.

Shaaran had brought the box of silks with her when they escaped, and ever since that time the silks had hung in the House of Books, to be marveled over and discussed endlessly by the people of the village.

Lann called for silence. Everyone turned to face her, and a tense hush fell.

"Friends," Lann said. "I ask you to listen carefully to what I have to say."

She spoke firmly, taking charge as she had done so often before. But it seemed to Rowan that her face had grown more haggard overnight and that she leaned more heavily on her stick. Rowan's step-father, Jonn of the Orchard, stood at her right hand, and Timon the teacher at her left. She looked frail between them.

"Our situation is grave," Lann said. "The store-house is almost empty, and the snow shows no sign of melting. Why this should be so—"

"It is a curse!" cried a voice from the center of the room. People turned, craning their necks to see who had spoken.

It was Neel the potter. His narrow face was pale and pinched. "A curse!" he repeated shrilly. "We have offended the Mountain, and now the Mountain has turned against us."

Rowan felt a chill that had nothing to do with his soaked boots or frozen fingers.

"That is foolish talk, Neel," said Jonn quietly.

"It is not!" cried Neel. "There has never been a winter such as this one. It is unnatural! Ask Timon if you do not believe me. Timon has examined the weather records. He knows I speak the truth."

All eyes now turned to Timon, who smoothed his gray beard nervously.

"This winter is certainly harsher than any we have had before," he said in his quiet, hesitating voice. "But there is no need to talk of curses. Our winters have been growing harder and longer for many years. And we must remember that we have lived in this valley for only three centuries. In a land as ancient as this, three hundred years are but the blink of an eye. Who can say what is natural and what is not? There is a Travelers' tale that tells of—"

Lann nudged him and he broke off, but it was too late. Neel was already nodding violently, his reddened eyes gleaming in the lamplight.

"Exactly!" Neel cried. "The tale of the Cold Time, when winter held the land in thrall, and ice creepers came down from the Mountain seeking warm flesh to devour!"

A chorus of jeers, led by Bronden the furniture maker, echoed through the room.

"Oh, I remember that one!" called Allun the baker. "My grandmother told it by the fire one winter's night when I was six years old. As I recall, I took my wooden sword to bed with me and lay awake for hours, waiting for the ice creepers to attack."

There was a ripple of laughter.

Neel bared his teeth. "You mock me, and ignore the message of the tale, at your peril!" he shouted. "Allun the baker is half Traveler himself, and should know better! Is he not always telling us that Travelers have roamed this land for almost as long as bukshah have grazed below the Mountain? And that Travelers' tales seem fanciful, but most are woven around a grain of truth?"

The laughter faltered and died.

"Neel is right!" quavered Solla the sweets maker, his soft chins wobbling as he spoke. "Remember the Valley of Gold! We thought *it* was just a Travelers' legend. Then its ruins were found on the other side of the Mountain. It was real enough once, and so were the people who lived in it, though they are long dead and gone."

The villagers murmured uncomfortably. The noise grew louder, quieting only when Lann held up her hand.

"The Travelers' Cold Time tale simply proves my point," said Timon firmly. "It proves that there is nothing unnatural about this cold. There has clearly been at least one long and terrible winter in the land before this—a season hard enough to have passed into legend. Now—"

"You are deliberately ignoring the most important thing, Timon!" Neel broke in shrilly. "In the tale, the Cold Time came because the people of the Valley of Gold turned their backs on the Mountain and failed to honor it. And we—we have done the same!"

He stabbed a trembling finger at the lengths of painted silk hanging behind Lann. "These images of another land and a time long gone have no place in our valley. They offend the Mountain. They must be burned!"

Rowan's stomach lurched. The room rang with shouts of shock and protest. Norris was red faced, his fists clenched. Even Shaaran had forgotten her shyness and was crying out. Norris and Shaaran had spent their lives guarding the silks in the land of the Zebak. The thought of the precious old paintings being destoyed was horrifying to them both.

"The silks are our history, Neel," said Lann, her gnarled hands tightening on her stick.

"No!" exclaimed Neel angrily. "Rin's story, the only story that matters, began the day our ancestors rose against their Zebak masters on this land's shore and began a new life."

He whirled around, appealing to his neighbors. "Our ancestors were brought to this land to help the Zebak conquer it, but instead the land gave them their freedom, and this valley became their home," he cried. "Once that history was all we knew, and it was enough for us!"

He turned and stared at Norris and Shaaran, his face sharp with dislike. "But ever since the silks and their guardians were brought here, all this has changed. Suddenly our minds are filled with questions about times long past and best forgotten. How long did our ancestors live as slaves in the land of the Zebak? Where did they come from at first? Is there another land, an even better land than this, which was once our own and perhaps could be so again?"

"It is natural for us to wonder, Neel," said Jonn. "There is no harm in it."

"There *is* harm!" Neel gestured wildly, his voice rising to a shriek. "Do you not see? By looking back, by questioning, we have rejected the Mountain's gift of life! And now the Mountain is offended and is taking its revenge!"

Jonn made a disgusted sound, and Timon shook his head.

"Never have I heard such foolishness!" snapped Lann, her faded eyes flashing with some of their old fire. "Be quiet, Neel, and let others with stronger heads than yours go on with the business for which this meeting was intended!"

Neel flushed and without another word pushed his way through the crowd and out of the room, slamming the door behind him. But Rowan could see that not everyone in the room agreed with Lann. Several people were glancing sympathetically after Neel. And Solla, for one, looked nervous.

Perhaps Lann could see this, too, and was

angered, for when she spoke again her voice was even harsher than it had been before.

"As I was saying, our situation is grave," she rasped. "By my calculation, the food remaining in the storehouse will feed us all for only twelve days more. And then only if we are very careful. The time has come to take action—action that I fear you will not like."

2 ∾ The Decision

The eyes of the crowd were fixed on Lann. She raised her chin. "It is my opinion that we should abandon the village and travel to the coast, where the Maris people and the Travelers will shelter and feed us until we can return," she said.

The room exploded in uproar.

"What?" shouted Bronden, her voice rising above the rest. "Are the people of Rin to become wandering beggars? And what do you think will happen to the village if we leave it now? If wind breaks windows that are not repaired? If snow buries the houses and roofs crack and fall in?"

Lann's wrinkled face tightened. "It is that or starve, Bronden," she said stiffly.

"Then I would rather starve!" snapped Bronden.

"Well, I would not!" called Marlie the weaver. She drew closer to Allun, her husband since the summer.

Allun took Marlie's hand in both his own and met Bronden's angry gaze.

"You may think it foolish, Bronden, but Marlie and I are more interested in living than dying," he said lightly. "Our child will be born before the month is out. We do not choose that it should come into the world only to perish."

Many people nodded, murmuring agreement. Others began exclaiming and arguing. Lann watched them with hooded eyes. Her shoulders had slumped and her knuckles were white as she gripped her stick.

Rowan's heart went out to her. She had done what she saw as her duty—what he, Jonn, and Timon had encouraged her to do—but it had cost her dearly.

"I urge you all to consider this plan with your minds rather than with your hearts," called Jonn, raising his voice to be heard over the tumult in the room. "We need only stay away until the danger is past. The Maris people and the Travelers are our friends and allies. They will help us gladly, as we would help them."

"Perhaps," said Bronden, her broad face creased in a frown. "But why must we go to the coast and leave our homes to be ruined by the snow and the wind? There must be another way. Where is Rowan of the Bukshah?" Her eyes raked the room.

Rowan shrank back into the shadows, but it was no use. "Ah, Rowan, there you are!" cried Bronden as she sighted him. "Why are you hiding there at the back of the room? You of all people—you who have saved Rin from disaster more than once— should be involved in this!"

Everyone turned to look as she pointed at Rowan.

Rowan felt his face grow warm. His confidence had grown greatly over the past few years, but he still did not enjoy being singled out. And the fact that some people in Rin believed that he had spe- cial, even magical, powers made him uncomfort- able. It was true that he had been able to save the village from danger in the past, but there had been nothing magic about what he had done. Magic of a kind had aided him, certainly—but not his own.

"Rowan, it is rumored that you have some strange bond—some linking of minds—with the Maris people's leader, the Keeper of the Crystal," growled Bronden. "If that is true, surely you could tell the Keeper of our trouble and ask him to send help?"

"And what of the Travelers, Rowan?" Solla called out. "You are respected by their chief, Ogden, are you not? And firm friends with Ogden's daughter, Zeel, who helped you save Annad from the

Zebak? Why do you not use the reed pipe they gave you to call for aid? The Travelers could carry supplies to the valley. We have shared our food with *them* often enough, when they have been camped here!"

Rowan wet his lips. "I fear that neither the Maris nor the Travelers can help us now, however much they might wish to," he said in a low voice.

"Of course they cannot!" snapped Lann. "*We* are the only people in this land who can survive the inland winter. You all know that! Or should. The Maris people and the Travelers always cling to the warmer coast, even in a normal cold season. This bitter chill would kill them long before they reached us."

Solla's face fell amid groans of disappointment from others in the room. Bronden simply folded her arms and exchanged somber glances with her neighbors.

"Very well," Lann said. "Now. I cannot force any person to leave. The journey to the coast will be long and filled with peril. The snow is deep, the cold is bitter, and the white wolves will be hungry on the plains. The protection and courage of every strong man and woman of Rin will be needed on the march if our weakest and youngest are to survive. But any journey, however perilous, is surely better than a slow and lingering death from starvation here."

The room was utterly silent. Lann's eyes swept over the crowd. Then she took a deep breath. "We will take a vote," she said. "Raise your hands if you agree with my plan."

Faces were grim, but a forest of hands went up. Only Bronden and a few very young children who did not understand what was happening remained still.

Rowan breathed a silent sigh of relief.

"Then it is decided," said Lann soberly. "The march to the coast will begin at first light tomorrow. I myself will divide the food remaining in the storehouse, so that everyone will have a fair share. As for the rest, pack only what you can carry on your backs, my friends, for the way will be hard and long."

"Surely the bukshah can carry—" Norris began, but Lann shook her head and glanced at Rowan.

This was the moment Rowan had been dreading. Feeling the eyes of the crowd upon him once more, he swallowed and forced himself to speak.

"The bukshah are too weak to travel as far as the coast," he said huskily. "They would perish on the journey."

"But they are dying now, one by one!" someone shouted. "If we leave them..."

Rowan's stomach churned. "The bukshah will not

be left alone," he said, aware of Shaaran and Norris listening intently beside him. "I will be staying with them."

Shaaran gasped in horror and looked around for Jiller, Rowan's mother. She expected Jiller to protest, to insist that her son escape from the village with them. But Jiller stood proudly silent at the front of the room, and Rowan's young sister, Annad, looked straight ahead without saying a word. Clearly they already knew of Rowan's decision and had accepted it.

"Most will survive no longer than a week or two," Rowan went on quietly. "But if I can keep just a few of the younger, stronger beasts alive until the weather changes, there is a chance that the herd will grow again in years to come."

Only those who knew him best could hear the misery in his level voice. Only they knew what it cost him to speak of even *one* of his beloved bukshah dying.

"No, Rowan!" Shaaran cried. Ignoring her brother, who was tugging at her sleeve in embarrassment, urging her to be still, she looked wildly around at the tall, serious-faced people who surrounded her.

"Tell him!" she pleaded. "Tell him he must not stay!"

"Rowan is the keeper of the bukshah," Lann said harshly. "The beasts know and trust him. His presence will comfort them and may help to keep them alive for a time even after their food is gone. You are a newcomer, girl, so perhaps you do not understand how important the bukshah are to Rin. Our whole way of life depends on them. Without them we would have no milk and cheese, no wool for clothing, no help in plowing the fields. Rowan's decision is the right one."

Shaaran shook her head disbelievingly. "How can that be? How can it be right for Rowan to be left here to die alone?"

Lann raised her head. "He will not be alone," she said. Her lips curving in a grim smile, she gestured at her stick. "Plainly I cannot walk unaided to the coast, and I do not choose to be a burden on the rest of you. So I, too, will be remaining."

"And I!" said Bronden stubbornly.

The harsh lines on Lann's face seemed to relax. Suddenly she looked very tired and old.

"That is all there is to say, then," she said. "Go to your homes now, and prepare."

The people turned silently toward the door.

"Wait!" Solla's quavering voice rose in the silence. "What of Sheba?"

Nervous whispers filled the room. Yes. What of Sheba the wise woman, Sheba the witch, crouched, mumbling, over the fire in her hut behind the orchard? Sheba, whose evil temper had been made even fouler by the cold? Sheba, who for weeks had remained hidden away, spitting jeers and taunts at all who dared approach her door, even those brave souls who had struggled through the snow to bring her food?

Did Sheba know of the plan to abandon the village? Almost certainly she did. She had a fearful way of knowing such things without a word being spoken in her presence.

The brave people of Rin shifted uncomfortably at the thought. Sheba could no more walk to the coast than Lann could. Would she remain behind, shaking her fist as they left her, cursing them for deserting her?

Or would she insist on being carried? Many a strong man shuddered at the thought of Sheba's bony arms hooked around his neck, her greasy rat-tails of hair swinging as she clung to his back like a giant spider, hissing at him to move faster.

John smiled grimly. "Sheba has not been forgotten," he said. "Jiller, Timon, and I all tried to gain entrance to her hut this morning, to speak to her. All of us were refused in turn and cursed for our pains. It seems there is only one person she wishes to see."

He looked toward Rowan.

Rowan's heart sank to his boots.

3 ∽ Sheba

Rowan trudged through the orchard, following the trail of deep footprints left by Jonn, Jiller, and Timon earlier in the day. He kept his head down. He did not want to look at the bare trees standing stark around him, their trunks smothered in whiteness, their twisted branches clawing at the gray sky like frozen skeleton fingers. He did not want to see Sheba's hut hunched ahead, half buried in snow, icicles fringing its low roof.

But he could not stop himself smelling the smoke of Sheba's fire, sour with ash and bitter herbs. He could not close his ears to the muffled sound of her voice, droning inside the hut, then stopping abruptly as he stepped into the flat, cleared space before her door.

It is foolish to feel this dread, he told himself as slowly he crossed the icy, trampled ground. I am not the young, fearful boy I was when I faced Sheba for the first time. Nothing she can do to me will make things worse than they are. Nothing she can tell me will be more terrifying than my own imaginings.

But still he shuddered, because he had learned that for all Sheba's malicious teasing, for all her delight in watching her chosen victims squirm, she always told the truth. And if her purpose in asking for him was to snuff out the last small flame of hope that still burned in his heart, he could not bear it.

There was no sound from the hut now. All was silence, except for the sound of the snow crunching beneath Rowan's boots.

At the door he closed his eyes for a moment, forcing himself to be calm. He was determined that this time, at last, he would meet Sheba without fear, and that her tricks would not dismay him. He raised his hand to knock.

Before his knuckles touched it, the door flew open, slamming back against the inside wall of the hut with a thundering crash. Icicles cracked and fell, plunging like spears into the snow behind Rowan's back. A gust of hot, sour air hit him full in the face. Gasping and choking, he recoiled, heart pounding, eyes stinging.

"Why do you stand there with the door gaping?"
Sheba shrieked from within. "All the good warm air
is escaping! Cowering fool of a boy! Make haste!"

Rowan stumbled across the threshold and into the
room. The door slammed shut behind him.

All was dark except for the fire, burning red with
flashes of green. Slowly Rowan's watering eyes
picked out the humped shape that was Sheba. She
had slumped back into her chair, which had been
drawn so close to the hearth that its feet were hidden by mounds of white ash.

"Come closer, Rowan of the Bukshah." The grating voice was deceptively gentle now. "Closer, but
not too close. Your skin is cold, and my heat is precious."

Clumsily Rowan moved forward, feeling as
though he was swimming through the thick, foul-
smelling dimness. Then, with a cry, he leaped back
as something huge and growling rose from the side
of the room and lunged at him. Sheba's spiteful
laughter rang in his ears as he fell sprawling onto
the filthy floorboards and twisted wildly, trying to
crawl to safety.

A burning, scaly nose nudged at his arm. Hot
breath scorched his cheek. Flat, yellow eyes stared
down at him, and leathery wings thumped the
floor, covering him with dust.

Rowan's blind panic vanished, to be replaced instantly by irritated shame. The attack had been no attack at all. He had merely been greeted by Sheba's companion, Unos the grach.

He crawled to his knees. The shock had left him weak. His hand was still shaking as he raised it to scratch Unos's shoulder. The scaly skin was not cool as he remembered but burning hot. The grach hissed with pleasure.

"Had you forgotten Unos, boy?" cackled Sheba with malicious delight. "Why, for shame! Did she not carry you and your idiot friends all the way home from the land of the Zebak only last summer?"

Rowan stood up, trying to ignore the pain in his bruised leg and shoulder.

"I had not forgotten Unos, Sheba," he said as calmly as he could. "But I did not expect her to be in here with you."

And why should I expect it? he thought as the grach's vast, mottled body swayed before him, radiating heat. Who would try to keep such a large creature indoors? Now that his eyes had adjusted to the light, he could see that there was no furniture in the room except for Sheba's chair. Everything had been cleared to make room for Unos.

"We have had work to do," Sheba said. She made a soft, twittering sound and Unos lumbered over to her, flopping down beside her chair. Sheba took a small stick from the bundle she held in her lap and tossed it into the fire.

The flames flickered green. The room seemed at once to become even hotter. The grach hissed contentedly and raised the spines on her back to their full height, the better to soak up the warmth.

Rowan wet his lips. "You wished to speak with me, Sheba?" he asked.

"Why would I wish to speak with *you*?" the old woman sneered. "Those fools in the village might think you are a great hero. *They* might think you have things of importance to say. But I know better. Oh, yes!" Her brown teeth gleamed in the firelight as she grinned.

Rowan said nothing. Sheba had done her best to shake him, and she had succeeded, but he was determined not to let her win this battle of nerves. The silence lengthened. The fire crackled. Rowan's head swam with the heat.

At last Sheba moved impatiently in her chair. "Do you dare play games with me, boy?" she said roughly. "Do you not know by now that I could crack you like a nut if I chose?"

She snorted as Rowan kept silence. "Have you begun to believe the tales they tell of you?" she sneered. "You dreamer! Why, without me you would be nothing. Nothing! You have always been nothing but my instrument, following *my* instructions."

"I know that, Sheba," Rowan said hastily, at the same time thinking that what she said was not quite true.

"Liar!" Sheba shouted, and Rowan's chest tightened as he realized that she had read his mind. As he began to stammer explanations, she spat viciously into the fire.

"Do you think I am a fool, that you try to flatter me, agreeing with me when you do not believe?" she demanded. "You are just like all the rest. Ungrateful and ignorant. Plotting and planning behind my back. Well, I will show you all!"

This sounded ominous. "Will—will you be leaving here in the morning with the rest, Sheba?" Rowan ventured.

"No, I will not!" she sneered. "Am I baggage, to be carried by floundering oafs? Now hold your chatter. I did not summon you here to speak *with* you, keeper of the bukshah, but to speak *to* you. Gather your poor wits and listen."

She leaned back in her chair, mumbling to herself, her clawlike hands clasped together at her throat. Slowly her eyelids drooped until her eyes were gleaming slits, shining first green, then white. Rowan's heart thudded painfully. The droning voice rose and fell, rose and fell, but he could not make out any words.

He took a step forward, but the heat—the heat of the fire, or of Sheba herself—was so intense that he gasped. Instinctively he tried to stumble back but could not move. The heat had caught and held him like a web of invisible fire. He struggled in its embrace, feeling it burning his skin, heating his blood, scorching his bones.

Then Sheba's mouth opened, and she began to speak clearly. The words came to Rowan on waves of scarlet heat. It was as though he saw them rather than heard them. They seemed to enter his eyes like burning brands, imprinting themselves on his brain.

"The beasts are wiser than we know
And where they lead, four souls must go.
One to weep and one to fight,
One to dream and one for flight.
Four must make their sacrifice.
In the realm twixt fire and ice
The hunger will not be denied,
The hunger must be satisfied.
And in that blast of fiery breath
The quest unites both life and death."

The voice trailed away. Sheba's mouth closed. The terrible words ringing in his mind, Rowan found himself staggering backward, out of the fiery haze.

Sheba's wrinkled eyelids slowly lifted. Her face was haggard with exhaustion.

"Well?" she mumbled.

"I—I do not understand," Rowan stammered.

"That is no business of mine," she snapped. "I have told you what I had to tell. The rest is your concern. I have another task to do, and do it I will, though I will have no thanks for it."

"Sheba, you must—" Rowan cried, but she waved him away irritably.

"Be still!" she ordered. "You are wasting my time, stealing my heat, and draining my strength."

She took a deep, rasping breath. When she began to speak again, she spoke rapidly, and all trace of spite had left her voice. For the first time in Rowan's life it was as if she was speaking to him as an equal.

"I cannot help you any further, Rowan of the Bukshah," she croaked. "All I know is that only you can do what must be done. All I can tell you is that everything you have learned until now has been preparation for this moment. All I can give you is...this."

She clutched at her throat again, fumbling at

something hidden under her ragged shawl. As she drew the object into the light, Rowan saw it was the strange old medallion she had given him to take to the land of the Zebak. It was hanging around her scrawny neck, still threaded on its faded cord of braided silk.

Rowan stared. He had forgotten all about the medallion. Certainly he did not remember giving it back to Sheba on his return to the village. But he must have, for there it was, clutched between her long yellow nails that curved like claws over its dull surface.

She lifted the cord from her neck and held out the medallion. "Take it!" she hissed. "Wear it. Learn what it is to be what I am."

Rowan hesitated. The last thing in the world he wanted to do was to obey. But his hand stretched out without his willing it, and before he could think the medallion was glowing warm between his fingers, and he was slipping the cord around his own neck. The medallion was heavy—far heavier than he remembered. It seemed to weigh him down.

Sheba slumped back into her chair, as if with relief.

"So—it is done," she muttered. "Go now. Unos and I must take in more heat yet. We must have all the fire has to give." She threw another stick into the fire. The flames crackled and burned green. Slowly she closed her eyes once more.

"But, Sheba, what am I to do?" asked Rowan desperately.

"Watch and wait," Sheba said without opening her eyes. "When it is time, you will know it."

Green light flickered on her sunken cheeks. She began to breathe slowly and deeply. Rowan knew that she would not speak to him again.

He left the hut like one walking in a dream. As the door closed behind him, freezing air rushed into his lungs and white light dazzled his eyes. Dazedly, the medallion hanging heavy as a great stone around his neck, he stumbled along the line of his own footprints to the orchard. As he stepped among the buried trees, he heard Sheba's muffled, droning chant begin once more.

4 ᴄ⌁ One to Dream

Rowan knew that Jiller, Jonn, and Annad would be waiting anxiously for him at home, but he deliberately slowed his steps as he left the orchard.

He was shaken and confused, but one thing was clear in his mind. Whatever else he said of his time in Sheba's hut, the words of her terrible rhyme must remain his secret.

Four must make their sacrifice.

If Jonn and Jiller heard those words, they would refuse to leave the village in the morning. It had been very difficult for Rowan to persuade them that they should join the march to the coast while he remained with the bukshah. Only when Lann had taken his side had they reluctantly agreed.

If they heard the rhyme, with its ominous talk of

beasts and sacrifice, they would change their minds again.

And that must not happen, Rowan thought desperately. The one thing that will help me bear what is to come is knowing that those I love—the *people* I love, at least—are safe.

But as he left the orchard and began toiling past the snowy drifts that covered the vegetable gardens, even that comfort began to fail him. In the distance he could see many people gathered by the storehouse. Lann was passing out shares of the remaining food. The bundles people were carrying away looked pitifully small.

Rowan's heart sank as he pictured the group setting off on the morrow, plowing toward the coast through deep, trackless snow, guided only by the sound of the buried stream.

The journey to Maris took at least a week at the best of times. How much longer would it take when every step was a battle? Three weeks? Four? Even longer? While slowly the food ran out, and cold, hunger, exhaustion, and the wolves took their toll.

Rowan felt a thrill of pure terror. Fighting it down, smothering the terrible imaginings that had caused it, he lowered his head and trudged on, hoping against hope that no one would turn and see him.

To his relief, he reached the first houses without

being hailed. He moved on toward the village square. As he passed Bronden's workshop, he heard the lonely sound of hammering. Bronden was working, stubbornly refusing to admit that soon there would be no one who needed her wares, trying to forget that soon only she, Lann, and Rowan would be left.

One to weep and one to fight,
One to dream and one for flight.

Bronden is the fighter, Rowan thought. And I am the useless dreamer, if Sheba is to be believed. Lann might weep tears of rage at her helplessness. But who is the fourth soul? The one who will run away?

Unwillingly his eyes turned to the pottery. The door was closed, the windows were shuttered, and no sound came from within. If Neel was there, he was keeping to himself.

Like a shadow, Rowan slipped through the deserted square and moved on. He peered through the window of the House of Books and saw that it, too, was empty. Only the silks stirred, gently billowing in the draft that blew beneath the door, so that the painted figures, trees, and animals seemed moving and alive.

Rowan's eyes were drawn to one particular scene—the one that had always affected him most powerfully. It pictured the slave village in the land of the Zebak, just over three hundred years ago. It showed Zebak guards tearing the bravest and strongest of the slaves from their weeping loved ones and locking them in iron cages.

Perhaps the people in that painted scene already knew that the strong ones were to be chained to the oars of fighting ships and forced to row across the sea to fight in the Zebak cause. But no one could guess that in the new land the slaves would turn against their masters and gain their freedom. No one could know that in their new life, in the peaceful Rin valley, they would not remember their past, because the Zebak had destroyed their memories. And no one could predict that the gentle souls left behind in slavery would gradually dwindle until, three hundred years later, only Shaaran and Norris remained to represent them.

Or perhaps, Rowan thought, there was one who *had* seen the future. In the midst of the confusion, a bent old woman, who had been painted holding a bundle of herbs to show that she was a wise woman and a healer, was secretly passing a medallion to a younger woman in one of the cages.

Rowan raised his fingers to the medallion hanging heavy around his neck. His memory of it had come flooding back now. It did not just *look* the same as the medallion in the painting. It *was* the same. It had come to the Rin valley with that young woman. It had been passed down through the generations of wise men and women who had followed her until it came into Sheba's hands.

And now Sheba has given it to me, Rowan thought. But not as she did before. In the land of the Zebak, she was with me in spirit. This time it is different. I feel it.

There was a roaring in his ears as he remembered Sheba's words.

Take it! Wear it. Learn what it is to be what I am.

His breath was misting the window. He could no longer see the billowing silks. But he made no effort to wipe the glass clean. He did not want to see the grave, intent faces of the two women, young and old, as something rare and powerful was passed between them. He did not want to think of what Sheba's gift meant.

Learn what it is to be what I am.

He turned from the window, made sure that the medallion and its cord were completely hidden under his clothing, and began walking rapidly away. Now he wanted to reach home as fast as he could. His face was burning, but his heart felt icy cold.

He covered the remaining distance quickly and soon was opening his own gate and hurrying down the cleared path to the house. Annad, who had plainly been watching for him, threw open the door before he reached it. She clasped his hand to draw him inside, then dropped it with a small shriek of surprise.

"Oh, you are hot!" she shrilled.

Rowan looked over her head to the anxious faces of Jonn and Jiller, who had left their packing and come to meet him.

"Sheba's fire was very warm," he said, pulling off his padded coat. "Far warmer than is natural. She has been weaving some sort of heat spell for herself and Unos, I think."

"No doubt we would be foolish to hope that she plans to share it with the rest of us," said Jiller dryly.

"I fear so," Rowan agreed. "She accused me of robbing her of heat, and it seems I did steal some, without knowing it."

He rubbed his hands together, only now realizing that they had not felt cold since he left Sheba's hut.

"What did she tell you, Rowan?" Annad demanded.

Rowan shrugged. "She was angry. She said she would not be leaving in the morning. She said we were ignorant and ungrateful and that she would show us all."

"*Show* us? What does she mean by that?" Jiller exclaimed.

"I do not know." Rowan slumped down at the table, which was cluttered with piles of folded blankets, food, and other supplies to be packed. "She did say she had something to do for which she would get no thanks, but she would not explain what she meant."

"Perhaps she is going to try to stop us from leaving," Jonn said.

"Perhaps." Rowan bent to unlace his boots. He had done what he had set out to do. Without telling a single lie, he had turned his family's attention away from him and toward Sheba's feelings about the forthcoming march to the coast.

It was a relief. But suddenly he felt very lonely, and terribly weary.

"I am sorry." He sighed. "I wish I could be of more help. But there is nothing more I can tell you."

That night it was colder than ever. No fresh snow fell, but by midnight the valley had filled with a strange, icy mist that chilled to the bone.

The people of Rin, packed and ready for the morrow, went silently to their rest, their minds and hearts numb with a dread few of them would admit, even to themselves. And in the darkness more than one remembered Neel's shrill voice rising in the crowded House of Books.

The Cold Time, when winter held the land in thrall and ice creepers came down from the Mountain seeking warm flesh to devour!

Rowan lay in his narrow bed, fully clothed, watching the shadows move sluggishly on the walls of his attic room as the candle burned low.

He no longer shared his room with Annad, who now slept in the small downstairs room Jonn and Jiller had built for her. Usually Rowan relished his privacy, and the extra space, but tonight the attic seemed very empty. He told himself that he should undress before the candle died. He told himself that he should try to sleep. But he could not find the energy to move.

The mist crawled at his window, white and smothering. He shuddered at the very sight of it, but at the same time he was glad of it, for it veiled his view of the brooding Mountain.

...the people of the Valley of Gold turned their backs on the Mountain and failed to honor it. And we—we have done the same!

Surely Neel had been speaking superstitious nonsense, as Lann had said. Surely . . .

On the stool beside Rowan's bed stood the golden owl he had found in the ruins of the Valley of Gold, on the other side of the Mountain. The owl gleamed in the flickering candlelight. Its emerald eyes seemed to glow as if they were trying to tell him something.

Rowan stretched out his hand to it. Its smooth surface seemed to warm under his fingertips.

The Valley of Gold was not destroyed by the Cold Time, he reminded himself. In the Travelers' tale, the people made their peace with the Mountain, and spring came again. The Valley did not meet its end until much later, centuries later, when it was overtaken by the killer trees of Unrin.

. . . the people made their peace with the Mountain . . .

But how? How?

Four must make their sacrifice.

Rowan's fingers tightened on the golden owl. Its green eyes seemed to flash.

The candle flickered, and went out.

Rowan opened his eyes in a place that was strange to him. It was cold and bleak. Snow covered the sloping ground, and the sky was dim but not yet dark. Cliffs towered above. He knew that he was on the Mountain.

Not far away, three cloaked and hooded figures were trudging through the snow in single file, following a well-trodden path that led upward. They were all carrying torches, the flames blowing and smoking in a bitter wind. The leader, tall and broad shouldered, was limping, leaning on a long stick. The second figure was small and delicate. The third was slight and of medium height.

This is the end . . .

The last figure in line paused, turned his head, and looked directly at Rowan. With a chill, Rowan recognized the face. It was the face he saw every time he looked into a mirror. The face stared at him, stared *through* him, as though he was invisible.

Rowan was outside himself. He was watching himself from a distance. But he could feel the emotions raging behind those glazed, unseeing eyes.

Fear. Anger. A terrible, aching grief.

I am dreaming, Rowan thought, and struggled to wake. But the dream was too real, too strong. It gripped him and held him helpless, forcing him to watch the scene before him, unable to move or speak.

The small middle figure stopped and turned. It was Shaaran. She was holding a long wooden box in her arms—the box of silks she had carried from the land of the Zebak.

"What is the matter?" the girl called in a low voice.

The Rowan figure shrugged. "I felt there was someone else here, watching us," he said.

The tall leader groaned impatiently, coming to a

stop and easing his injured leg. "How could there be?" he growled. "We are the only ones left."

It was Norris, his handsome face tight with strain, his eyes haunted. "The only ones left," he repeated, and suddenly gave a bark of harsh laughter.

Shaaran glanced at him, her brow wrinkled anxiously. "The light is failing," she said, clutching the box more tightly. "We must move on. We must follow the beasts."

Norris looked around and laughed again. "What is the point?" he said loudly. "What can it matter where we die?" Dropping the stick, he flung himself to the ground.

Shaaran ran to him, and Rowan saw himself move quickly to join her. Together they pulled at Norris's arms. Norris lay where he was, sprawled amid the churned mud and snow, his body racked again and again with gales of that terrible laughter.

"Get up," Rowan heard himself say, in a calm, determined voice he would not have recognized as his own. "We will not leave you. But if we stay here we will *all* die, to no purpose. And when the others return from the coast—"

"They will never return," Norris wheezed, between gasps of laughter that were more like sobs. "They are all dead by now, I am sure of it, and the wise woman with them. Do you not understand?

We are finished. This is the end."

This is the end . . .

Shaaran opened her mouth as if to scream. But when the sound came it was very faint, as though Rowan was hearing it from far away. A mist was closing over his eyes—

He woke choking, his heart pounding. He was burning hot, bathed in sweat.

He tumbled out of bed. Shaaran's scream was still echoing in his mind as he stumbled to the window and flung it open. He leaned out into the night, taking deep, gasping breaths. The mist swirled around his head, thick and icy cold.

Learn what it is to be what I am.

No! Rowan told himself desperately, digging his fingers into the rough wood of the sill. It was nothing but a stupid dream! There was nothing real about it. How could I climb the Mountain with Shaaran and Norris? They are going to the coast with the rest, in the morning.

Then his heart gave a great thud, for suddenly the scream he had heard in his dream came again, muffled by the mist but high and full of terror.

And this time there was no doubt that it was real.

5 ∞ Shocks

Rowan pounded down the stairs. He pulled on his boots and coat, which had been left drying by the glowing embers of the fire, and hurtled out into the night. He heard Jonn, Jiller, and Annad stirring and calling out. He shouted back to them, but did not stop.

There was no time. He was sure that the voice he had heard was Shaaran's, and Shaaran would not have screamed like that unless she was in dire need.

The mist was like a white blanket in front of his eyes. Arms outstretched before him, he felt his way to the garden gate and stumbled blindly on. For a few long moments there was utter silence. Then, from somewhere ahead, there was a crash, Shaaran's voice desperately crying for help, and another voice, high pitched and gabbling.

And now he could see a flickering light—a flame—wavering faintly through the mist. Recklessly he began to run.

Other people had woken now. Rowan could hear voices raised in questioning and alarm and the sounds of doors and windows opening. But he knew he was closer to the trouble than anyone else.

He could not understand a word of the frenzied gabbling that still mingled with Shaaran's cries, but its squealing tone was only too familiar, and the sight of the wavering flame gave him grim warning of what he was about to find.

Sure enough, when he reached the House of Books, the door was gaping wide, and light and shadows leaped within. Shaaran, her fragile figure unmistakable even in the dimness, was struggling with a dark figure at the back of the room. And somewhere there was fire!

Shouting, Rowan flung himself through the doorway and nearly tripped over a body lying motionless on the floor. He staggered back. Flames threw dancing light on the unconscious face.

It was Norris. His head was pressed against the base of a tall shelf of books. His eyes were closed, his brow wet with blood. A flaming torch lay beside his hand, as if he had dropped it when he fell. The floorboards beneath the torch were smoking, and some of the books in the shelf were already alight, flames licking greedily upward, fanned by the draft from the door.

Rowan snatched up the torch and held it high. Now he could see Shaaran clearly. And he could see the struggling man she was clinging to with all her strength. It was Neel the potter, his pale face twisted with rage as he fought to free himself. Rowan took a step forward.

"No!" screamed Shaaran. "The fire, Rowan! Put out the—"

With a piercing squeal of rage, Neel made a final, violent effort, threw her aside, and sprang at Rowan. Rowan caught a glimpse of his frenzied face, eyes wild, teeth bared, lips flecked with foam. Then Neel was upon him, wrestling him to the ground, trying to tear the torch from his hand.

"Let go!" Neel snarled. "Give it to me! The silks must burn! I must burn them and save us all!"

"No!" Rowan panted, clutching the torch as Neel's strong fingers tried to break his grip. He knew he would not be able to hold on much longer.

He twisted his head around until he could see the door and made his eyes widen as if in surprise and relief.

"Jonn!" he shouted. "Help me!"

Neel's attention faltered, and his grip loosened as

he, too, looked at the door. Only for an instant, but it was enough. Rowan tore his arm free and hurled the torch through the open doorway into the snow.

Neel gave a high wail and sprang after it. His head spinning, Rowan staggered to his feet and kicked the door closed. He tore off his coat and began using it to beat at the fire in the bookshelf. Many books were smoldering now. Small, hungry flames were running like insects along the rows. The room was full of smoke.

"Shaaran, get out!" he shouted.

Receiving no reply, he glanced around fearfully. Through a thick veil of smoke he saw, to his amazement, that Shaaran was standing on a table at the end of the room. She had her back to him, and was rapidly taking down the silks, rolling them up, and piling them into their wooden box.

Rowan called again, but Shaaran did not turn. She was so intent on her task that he doubted she could even hear him. The smoke was growing thicker by the moment. As he watched, she began to cough and choke.

"Shaaran!" he bellowed.

The door crashed open behind him. He whirled around, terrified that Neel had returned. Then a wave of relief flooded through him as he saw, wreathed in mist that mingled with the smoke, the shocked faces

of Jonn, Jiller, and Bronden, with a crowd of others
behind them. Jonn was holding a glowing lantern.

"It was Neel!" Rowan gasped. "He tried to burn
the silks. He has run away. Out there . . . "

His face darkening with anger, Jonn turned and
disappeared into the mist. Bronden ran after him.
The others began calling for blankets and water.

Leaving them to see to the fire, and to Norris,
Rowan wound his scarf around his mouth and nose
and plunged into the thick smoke at the back of
the room.

He found Shaaran a few steps from the table. The
box of silks was clutched in her arms, but, over-
come by the smoke at last, she had fallen to her
knees. Rowan pulled her to her feet and began
dragging her toward the door.

"I could not sleep." The words burst from Shaaran
in choking, sobbing gasps. "I feared for the silks. So
at last Norris and I came to take them, and—and
we saw a light, and it was Neel. We were . . . just in
time. He was about to . . . Norris took the flame,
and they fought, but then Neel pushed him, and he
fell and hit his head . . . "

"Be still now, Shaaran. Norris is safe," Rowan said
soothingly. "And the silks are safe also."

But a cold hand closed on his heart as they
plunged at last into the swirling chill of the outside

air and saw Norris, wrapped in a blanket, leaning heavily on Allun's shoulder. Norris's eyes were glazed, and he was sweating with pain as he tried to stand on a leg that clearly would not support him.

He had suffered more than a blow on the head. His leg had been injured when he fell. He would not now be leaving the village in the morning with the others. He could not possibly make the journey to the coast. And Shaaran would not leave her brother. Nothing was more certain.

This still does not mean the dream was a prophecy, Rowan told himself dazedly as Shaaran broke away from him and stumbled to Norris's side. It does not!

He became aware that the bukshah were bellow-ing. They had been disturbed by the shouting and the smell of fire, no doubt. Or perhaps Neel had run toward them and startled them.

In their present restless state, this could be disas-trous. Rowan knew that they could break down their fence again and bolt if nothing was done to calm them. Pushing his way through the crowd, he began to walk swiftly toward the bukshah field.

To his relief the strange mist had thinned, so he could see the familiar way well enough, even with-out a light. As he walked he thought. And the more he thought, the more convinced he became that it was simply a coincidence that Norris and Shaaran would be staying in the village.

Those hooded cloaks we were wearing in my dream—why, they were old Rin warrior cloaks, made of bukshah skin, he told himself. There are no cloaks like that in Rin anymore. And besides, in the dream Norris said that Sheba had gone to the coast. That will *certainly* not happen. Sheba told me so herself.

The bukshah were still calling, Star's distinctive low bellow louder than all the rest. Rowan quickened his pace. He was almost running by the time he reached the gate to the field.

Beside the gate was the shed where the herd's winter feed was stored. Rowan threw open the shed door, plunged into the sweet-smelling darkness inside, and grabbed a half bale of hay from the edge of the sadly small stack remaining on the floor. He knew that a little food would calm the great animals more quickly than anything.

Heaving the bale after him, he let himself into the field and called softly.

The bellowing ceased, but the bukshah did not come to him. Puzzled, Rowan peered through the darkness and the mist that still rolled thickly over the frozen stream, then he called again.

He could hear Star rumbling in reply, but still there was no movement. Rowan trudged toward the sound, moving upward, and at last saw humped gray shapes standing motionless against the fence that separated the field from the orchard. Here the mist was just a faint veil, and soon he could see the herd clearly.

The bukshah were crowded together in a tight group, the largest and strongest on the outside, the weaker ones in the center. Even when they saw what Rowan was carrying, none of them moved except Star, who took a single step forward.

"Star, there is no need to fear," Rowan crooned as he reached her and dropped the bale of hay at her feet. He patted her gently. "Neel would not harm you, and the fire is out. You are safe."

Star shook her great head, rumbling deep in her throat. Her skin was twitching beneath the curled wool of her mane. Rowan felt an unpleasant twinge of doubt.

Were the bukshah safe? Star certainly did not seem to think so, and Rowan was uncomfortably aware that her instincts had proved more reliable than his in the past.

Rapidly he counted heads. Then, a cold feeling growing in his chest, he moved among the great beasts, calling them by name. They all answered him but one. Pale gray Twilight, the oldest, shaggiest bukshah in the herd, Lann's favorite, was missing. And there could be only one reason for that.

Fighting despair, Rowan bent to tear the bale apart so that the herd could share it. "I am sorry, Star," he said. "I am sorry about Twilight. I did not realize she was—so weak. In the morning I will find her. For now—"

"Rowan! Is that you?"

Rowan jumped. It was Strong Jonn's voice, sounding oddly strained, coming from the direction of the orchard.

Rowan peered over the fence. Dimly he saw the glow of a lantern. "Yes, Jonn!" he shouted.

"Rowan, come here!"

There was no mistaking the strangled tone in Jonn's voice now. What had happened? Was it something to do with Neel?

His heart in his mouth, Rowan gave Star a final pat, scrambled over the fence, and waded through the snow toward the lantern's light.

He found Jonn waiting for him among the first of the half-buried trees. The big man looked distracted, but his eyes widened in shock as Rowan appeared from the darkness.

"Rowan!" he gasped. "Where is your coat? You must be frozen!"

Only then did Rowan realize that he had left his coat on the floor in the House of Books. He had walked to the bukshah field with no protection other than his woolen jacket. And he had not even noticed.

He and Jonn gaped at each other for a long moment. Then Jonn shook his head violently, as if to clear it.

"It is all part of the same thing!" he muttered to himself. Abruptly he beckoned to Rowan. "Come and see!" he ordered. "See what I found when I was searching for Neel."

He turned and strode off through the trees. Wondering, Rowan followed, then his stomach began to churn as he realized that Jonn was making for Sheba's hut.

At the edge of the orchard Jonn stopped and held up his lantern. Ahead was the cleared space that lay before Sheba's door.

But it was not as it had been when Rowan saw it last. No flickering light shone from the hut. There was no smell of bitter smoke. No sound of chanting. And a broad black path led away from the door, curving across the trampled snow and on to the hills beyond.

Rowan stared. "What is it?" he whispered.

Without a word Jonn led him to the black path. As he stepped upon it, Rowan could feel heat rising from the ground, even through his thick, wet boots. He took a few steps, and with wonder saw steam rising where he trod.

"The path goes right through the hills," said Jonn, his usually calm voice taut with excitement. "I followed it until I was sure. It meets the stream, then continues, toward the coast."

Rowan stared, unable to take it in. He swallowed painfully. "But Sheba told me—"

"Nothing but the truth!" Jonn broke in. "In her own spiteful, deceiving way she told you exactly what she planned. She said she would show us, and she *is* showing us! She said she would not be leaving the village with us and she will *not*. Because she has already gone! She is *leading* us!"

He gripped Rowan's arm. "Do you not see, Rowan? This is what the heat spell was intended to do. Sheba is going to blaze a path through the snow, all the way to the coast!"

"But . . . " The word seemed to stick in Rowan's throat. He was choking with mingled astonishment, relief, and fear. "But Sheba can barely walk, Jonn! Even if she could melt the snow, how could she . . . ?"

"She is not walking, but riding," said Jonn. He held his lantern low so that its light flooded the black ground. And there, unmistakable, were the heavy tracks of a huge, clawed beast.

The tracks of Unos the grach.

6 ⌒ Grim Discoveries

And so it was that the people of Rin left their valley at dawn, not struggling through deep snow as they had expected, but tramping four abreast along the burned black trail that their wise woman had left for them to follow.

Rowan and Shaaran farewelled them at the place where the black trail met the stream, then stood watching as they marched away. The people's heads were high and their eyes were fixed on the horizon. Their hearts were full, but they did not weep, and only Allun, the half Traveler, looked back.

"They do not care," murmured Shaaran. Her eyes were brimming with tears.

"They do," said Rowan. "But it is not their way to show it." He returned Allun's wave, then turned away so he could no longer see the long line traveling east, the only moving thing in a wilderness of white.

"Come," he said, putting his arm around Shaaran's shoulders. "We must get back to the others. Norris will be wondering where you are."

Shaaran bit her lip. "No, he will not," she said in a low voice. "He is very angry because I would not leave him. He says my weakness shames us both. But except for our grandfather, Norris was my only companion in the land of the Zebak. I could not abandon him, Rowan. I could not!"

Rowan felt sorry for her. He knew only too well how it felt to be the weakling, the different one, among the sturdy people of Rin.

"You are not weak, Shaaran," he said as they began to walk back toward the village. "You are strong, in your own way. Look at how you struggled with Neel to protect the silks!"

Immediately he wished he had not spoken, for Shaaran winced at the sound of Neel's name. The potter had not been found the night before, despite a search that had lasted for hours.

"The fool has fallen into a hole and been frozen, you may count on it," Lann had said flatly.

But Rowan and Jonn had not been so sure. And Shaaran was haunted by the fear that Neel was lurking somewhere in the village, waiting his chance to strike at the silks again.

"I do not blame Neel," she said. "He only tried to do what he thought was right, and I hope with all my heart he is safe. But if only he could be found! Then we could talk to him, explain to him. . . ."

Rowan glanced at her. He hoped she would not repeat these forgiving words in front of Lann. The old warrior would greet them with withering contempt.

As they passed Sheba's hut and began tramping through the orchard, Rowan thought of something that might turn Shaaran's mind from her troubles.

"I must feed the bukshah," he said. "Will you come with me?"

Shaaran hesitated, a mixture of fear and the wish to please warring on her face. It had always amazed Rowan that she could fear the gentle bukshah, while Unos the grach, hideous and clawed, did not frighten her at all.

"Never mind," he said quickly. "I should report to Lann first, in any case, or she will fret. But the bukshah would never harm you, Shaaran. They are the gentlest of beasts."

"Their horns look very dangerous," Shaaran said in a small voice.

Rowan laughed. "I have told you—they never use

their horns," he said. "Not even on another."

"Why do they have horns at all, then?" Shaaran retorted.

Rowan could find no answer to that. He had often wondered the same thing himself.

The village was eerily silent when they entered it. They did not speak as they moved through the square, instinctively creeping on tiptoe past the barred and shuttered houses. Without people to give it life, the place seemed like a graveyard.

It was with relief that they reached the bakery, for there, at least, there was noise and movement. As Rowan and Shaaran entered the big kitchen, they heard Lann's voice barking instructions and the sound of furniture being moved around in the living room beyond.

It had been decided that to make the small supplies of wood and oil last as long as possible, the people remaining in Rin should move into one dwelling, so they could share food, light, and warmth.

Lann had decided on the bakery because it was large and close to the village center. Rowan was glad. He loved the bakery, filled for him with pleasant memories of Allun's cheerful mother, Sara, and of Allun himself singing as he pulled trays of fragrant buns and rolls from the old black oven.

But when he and Shaaran walked into the cozy

living room behind the kitchen, he realized that with Lann in charge, life at the bakery would not be as friendly and comfortable as it had been with Sara as the homemaker.

The large room had been cleared of furniture. The only pieces remaining were one chair before the fire, where Norris sat, scowling furiously, and the stool on which his injured leg was propped.

Rugs brought from the bedchambers upstairs overlapped one another all over the floor to exclude drafts. The windows were closely shuttered. Bronden was blocking the staircase with furniture and old blankets to prevent warm air rising to waste.

Five sets of rolled bedding had been ranged neatly around the bare walls. Each person's bag of belongings had been placed beside his or her bedroll, and on the floor next to this were a tin mug, a plate, and a spoon.

It was like an army camp fitted out for a siege—a siege against the cold. Lann stood in the midst of it, hunched over her stick.

"So! Here you are at last!" she said as Rowan and Shaaran appeared. "See how much we have had to do while you two have been lollygagging in the hills? This is not a good way to begin!"

Her tone was harsh, her face a mass of frowning

lines. Rowan felt Shaaran shrink back against him and sighed inwardly. He knew only too well that Lann was using work and anger to cover the misery she felt at the departure of her people. But to Shaaran the old woman seemed merely stern and frightening.

"Help Bronden with the stairs, Rowan of the Bukshah," snapped Lann. "You, girl, can fetch more wood for the fire."

"I can do that," Norris said, struggling to rise. "Shaaran is not strong enough to—"

"Stay where you are, Norris!" barked Lann. "If you do not rest your leg, it will not heal. Your sister insisted on staying, and she must earn her keep."

Sulkily Norris sank back into his chair.

"I cannot help Bronden just now, Lann," Rowan said. "I must tend the bukshah." He took a deep breath and forced himself to go on in the same level voice as before. "I may be a little longer than usual. Twilight died last night. I need to find her, and cover her for the sake of the others."

"Twilight?" The lines on Lann's face seemed to deepen, and for a moment something like despair darkened her faded eyes. But all she said was, "Cover her, then. But do not forget to shear her first. The wool must not be wasted."

● ● ●

The bukshah field was a silent wasteland of white, brown, and gray. Behind it loomed the vast bulk of the Mountain, shrouded in mist.

The bukshah were still crowded together against the orchard fence. The snow around them was pocked with the holes they had dug to uncover grass roots, the only food still available to them in their field.

They did not come to Rowan when he called them, and even when he broke the ice on their pool with an iron spike, they did not stir. Only when he hurried to the shed and hauled out their daily ration of hay did they move toward him.

When they had all begun to eat, Rowan picked up the spade, the sack, and the shears he had laid ready and followed the tracks of stampeding hoofs down to a large, trampled patch of ground beside the snow-covered stream.

To his surprise there was no sign of Twilight's body anywhere.

The ice-bound stream gurgled secretly beneath his feet as he crossed the snow that covered it. The Mountain hulked before him, a shapeless wall of swirling white. Cold streamed from it, catching Rowan in the face like icy breath, making him gasp.

He recoiled in shock. Neel's shrill voice echoed in his memory.

It is a curse! . . . We have offended the Mountain, and now the Mountain has turned against us.

Then Rowan saw something that, in the past few, frantic days, he had not noticed before.

There were no bukshah tracks on this side of the stream. Long, smooth drifts of snow, rising one beside the other like waves on the sea of Maris, ran all the way to the mists of the Mountain. Even in their ceaseless quest for food, the bukshah had not crossed the stream since the last snowfall, three days ago.

Rowan jumped violently as a soft grunting rumble sounded behind him. He whirled around and saw Star standing on the other side of the stream, watching him. As an experiment, he held out his hand, inviting her to come to him, but she tossed her heavy head and would not stir.

Dragging the spade behind him, Rowan crossed the stream again and moved to her side. He plunged his gloved hands into the thick wool of her mane and felt her skin trembling beneath.

"Star, where did Twilight fall?" he whispered.

Star pawed the ground, her head lowered, the points of her great curved horns almost touching the snow.

"Twilight!" Rowan repeated, gripping her mane more tightly. "Show me, Star."

Star turned her head to look at him. Then, reluctantly, she began to move.

She led Rowan along the hidden stream until she reached the farthest corner of the trampled space. There she stopped and pawed the ground again.

Rowan looked about him. There was nothing to see but a great snowdrift that bridged the stream and ended in a tumbled pile at the edge of the space.

A horrible idea came to him. Perhaps Twilight had fallen to her knees and the end of the drift had collapsed over her as she struggled to rise. His eyes burned at the thought. Dashing the tears away before they could fall and freeze on his cheeks, he took the spade and began digging in the pile of snow.

Star backed away, rumbling urgently.

"Do not fear, Star," Rowan said. Yet with every spadeful of snow he cast aside, his own fear grew greater. His hands were shaking.

What is the matter with me? he thought angrily. I have seen death before, many times. Gritting his teeth, he bent his back and shoveled more strongly, tunneling into the mass of frozen white.

Then suddenly, with a cry of shock, he lurched forward, stumbling and almost falling. The spade had plunged into emptiness. Into a hollow beneath the snow.

Dropping to his knees, Rowan peered into the hollow. His skin crawled.

A long, narrow, blue-shadowed space. The loud gurgling of the stream, echoing from icy walls. Dead air, so chill that it stung his lips and eyes, so cold that the medallion around his neck seemed to burn.

Rowan gaped, hypnotized by the strangeness, frozen with dread. Star moaned, nudging him, urging him to rise. Her touch broke the spell. Slowly his eyes adjusted to the light, and his mind made sense of what he was seeing.

The tumbled snow had masked the entrance to a tunnel beneath the snowdrift. At the far end, jammed between frozen walls, lay something shaggy and gray.

Twilight.

A lump rose in Rowan's throat. He thought he could see what had happened. As he had feared, Twilight had fallen and been buried by collapsing snow. Somehow she must have dragged herself forward, creating a tunnel through the icy whiteness as she went. Then at last, when she could go no farther, she had simply laid down her head and died.

Trembling, he crawled to his feet. The thought of uncovering Twilight's pathetic remains and taking her wool filled him with revulsion. The thought of breaking into that icy, blue-shadowed tomb filled him with dread. He knew he could not do it.

He snatched up the spade and with a few strokes closed the mouth of the tunnel, sealing it once more.

Star nudged his arm roughly, anxious to be gone. Rowan took hold of her mane again and let her lead him away. Beneath her thick coat her skin still twitched, twitched.

The beasts are wiser than we know. . . .

Rowan's fingers tightened in the soft wool as a terrible knowledge pierced his mind like a shard of ice.

Star loved him, but she no longer trusted him to make decisions for her. She knew that the cold was coming from the Mountain. She had known it for days. She knew that all Rowan's care and comfort could only lead to a slower way for the herd to die.

As if she sensed Rowan's despair, the great buk-shah stopped and lifted her head to look at him. She held his gaze for a long moment, her small black eyes searching his. Rowan stared back helplessly. And at last Star looked away again, and plodded on.

The rest of the day passed like a dream—a strange, almost silent dream. The only sound was Bronden hammering, doggedly sealing one cottage after another against the weather.

Rowan said nothing of his discoveries in the buk-shah field. He did not wish to speak of Twilight's strange and horrible death. Neither was he ready to speak of his terror when he felt the icy breath of the Mountain upon his face. If he told the others that the terrible cold that gripped the land was flowing from the Mountain, he would sound as hysterical and superstitious as Neel.

He spent the rest of the morning doing Lann's bidding, carrying food, fuel, and other needs to the bakery, searching vainly for a misplaced lantern, which Lann insisted had been newly filled with oil and could not be spared. In the afternoon, after a meager meal of bread and cheese, he worked in the bukshah field, checking the fences, breaking the ice on the pool again while the herd watched him listlessly.

As the light dimmed, it grew colder. Colder than ever before. Rowan worked on. He kept his eyes lowered so that he would not have to look at the Mountain. But every nerve in his body was aware of it looming above him, breathing cold, breathing death.

By the time the Dragon on the Mountain's peak roared at dusk, his hands were so numb that he could no longer hold his tools. Mist was thickening at the base of the Mountain, stealing across the snowdrifts toward the stream. He knew he had to seek the shelter of the bakery, and quickly. But he did not want to leave the bukshah, huddled together by the orchard fence. He dreaded what the night would bring.

7 ∾ Night Terrors

Rowan crept through the shadowed, empty streets, past the shuttered houses, feeling like a ghost. But when finally he reached the bakery and let himself into the warm, lighted kitchen, his spirits lifted a little.

A pot of soup, thin but fragrant with herbs, was simmering on the stove. In the living room beyond, all was peace. Norris was showing Bronden how to knot rope in a way that was new to her. Lann was dozing by the fire. And Shaaran was standing before a piece of silk stretched on a frame, a fine brush in her hand.

"Lann said I should make a silk of this time—of the snow and the people leaving the village," she explained to Rowan as he joined her. "She said it was something useful I could do. She said that I must carry on the work of my ancestors, painting the important events in our history so that those who come after will not forget. I have nearly finished the outlines already."

Rowan looked with admiration at the clever sketch—the long, long line of people following a black road winding east, the bukshah in their field, the Mountain towering above all. Then he met Shaaran's eyes, no longer dull and despairing but filled with purpose, and blessed Lann for thinking of the one thing that might comfort her.

He went to his hard bed early that night. He did not want to talk. He had too much on his mind that he could not share. But though he was weary, he fought against sleep.

He lay with his face to the wall while Shaaran painted and Lann, Bronden, and Norris murmured by the fire, speaking of the people who were gone, wondering how far they had traveled this day and if they were safe.

Slowly the voices grew dim, until they were a soft buzzing somewhere at the edge of his consciousness. He closed his eyes and made himself relax.

You need not fear, he told himself. You will not dream this time. You will not dream. . . .

Rowan opened his eyes. He was in a cave. Mist

swirled in the darkness beyond the narrow, ragged triangle of the cave's mouth. Beside him, three figures wrapped in heavy cloaks huddled by a tiny fire. The flickering red light showed their faces only dimly, but Rowan saw enough to know who they were. Norris. Shaaran. Himself.

The three paid no attention to him. He knew they could not see him. This time he knew at once that he was dreaming.

"The fire will keep us safe," Shaaran whispered. "Surely it will."

"It should," Norris said gruffly. "But the night will be long."

Rowan watched his mirror image glance at the girl. Her eyes were dark with fear. The box of silks was on her lap. She was clutching it so tightly that her fingers were white.

"Let us look at some of the silks," the Rowan figure suggested gently. "Let us think of old times. It will take our minds from the present and remind us why we are here."

Norris snorted and turned away, but the girl nodded gratefully. She opened the box, revealing the familiar rolls of silk. She dug deep, pulled one out at random, then stood up and let it unroll. The Rowan figure caught his breath. Norris spun around. The girl looked down, saw what the picture was, and exclaimed in dismay, "Oh, what ill fortune! I did not mean . . . "

Her voice trailed away as with trembling hands she began to roll the painting up again. But Rowan had seen enough to make the hair rise on the back of his neck.

The painting was all in white, black, and shades of blue and gray. The shapes upon it were clear and precise, the creations of a skillful hand.

A long line of people trekking away through snow-covered hills, following a burned black path that wound toward a bleak horizon. Bukshah, the only dark objects in a white wasteland, clustered together beneath the Mountain, which loomed over all, wreathed in mist.

And writhing from the mist, in their hundreds, in their thousands, huge white snakelike things with no eyes. Things with gaping blue-lined jaws and teeth like shards of ice. Things that slid and twisted out of the cold, things that tunneled through the snow, seeking, seeking—

Something gripped Rowan's arm. He jerked in shock, tried to shake it off. He tried to scream, but all he could manage was a strangled groan.

"Rowan!" The voice was loud in his ear. It was Bronden's voice, harshly whispering. "Wake! You are thrashing about and moaning in your sleep, disturbing all of us. Wake, or be still, for pity's sake!"

Rowan's eyes flew open. For a split second he lay still, panting, looking up at Bronden's puffy, irritated face. Then he sprang up, nearly knocking her off her feet.

"What is the matter with you?" she cried angrily.

Rowan's throat was tight with fear, his head spinning with the visions of the dream.

"The bukshah!" he choked, frantically pulling on his boots, snatching up his knife. "I have been wrong! So wrong! Star knew—they all knew . . . ah, poor Twilight! She was the first. Seized and dragged under. Dragged . . . "

Bronden gaped at him. In the dim light of the fire he could see Lann slowly sitting up, Norris and Shaaran staring.

The fire will keep us safe.

Rowan ran to the other side of the room, pulled a torch from the pile and plunged it into the coals of the fire. It caught quickly.

"Rowan!" Lann barked, holding out an arm impatiently so that Bronden could haul her to her feet. "Report!"

"Bring torches!" Rowan shouted. "The bukshah field! Make haste, for pity's sake!"

Holding his flame high, he darted through the

kitchen and out into the street, where the freezing mist swirled like a living thing, catching at his clothes, rushing into his lungs, blinding him.

But he ran despite it, heart pounding, chest aching with fear. He could hear Bronden's heavy footfalls behind him. Lighter steps, too, behind Bronden. And Norris roaring to Shaaran to come back, to stay in safety. And Lann shouting fruitless orders after them all.

As he burst from among the houses and plunged down toward the silent bukshah field, Rowan glanced over his shoulder and saw the torches flickering through the mist. Four bobbing torches, strung out in a line.

One to weep and one to fight,
One to dream and one for flight.

And suddenly, very near, there was an earsplitting shriek.

Not Star. Nor any of the other bukshah. No beast had made that sound. That was a human voice, floating through the mist on waves of deathly cold.

The outline of the feed shed loomed ahead. Its door was gaping wide. Beside it a section of fence lay flattened, half buried in trampled snow. And very near, in the bukshah field, was a wildly moving light.

"Ah, no! No!" The sobbing scream rose, high and wailing.

Rowan stumbled forward, over the ruined fence. And through the mist he saw Neel the potter, slipping and staggering backward in the snow. Neel was screaming, scrambling back toward the feed shed, swinging a blazing lantern in great arcs in front of his body.

Wisps of hay stuck in Neel's hair, on his clothes. The mist was swirling around him, above him, making writhing white shapes in the lantern light. His eyes were wide and staring, his twisted face turned upward, a gleaming mask of terror.

Neel is not dead, Rowan found himself thinking blankly, stupidly, as his mind grappled with what his eyes were seeing. It was Neel who took Lann's lantern. Neel has been hiding in the feed shed, behind the bales of hay, all this time. But what is he . . . why is he . . . ?

Neel shrieked, swinging the lantern high. Then Rowan, with a thrill of terror, saw at last what the potter could see. Saw what the shapes were that twisted and loomed just beyond the circle of light.

Surrounding Neel, towering over him, were three huge, hideous, white, snakelike beasts, their blunt, eyeless heads jabbing downward, their gaping mouths like blue-shadowed holes in snow.

Neel screamed again, burning oil spilling from the lantern as he swung it above his head. Liquid fire spattered on his hands, fell sizzling on the snow. The lunging beasts hissed, and the icy cold of their breath seemed to freeze the very air so that it thickened and went white. Neel fell flat on his back, the sweat on his face frozen into a pale, cracked mask, the lantern still clutched in his hand.

Without thinking, Rowan shouted and leaped forward, the flaming torch held high above his head. He slithered down toward Neel, reaching for him desperately. But now Neel was screaming again, writhing on the icy ground. Rowan seized his arm, trying to drag him up. Wildly Neel clutched at him, pulling him to his knees.

"They have come for us!" Neel shrieked. "Now do you believe? Now do you see?"

"Get up!" shouted Rowan, struggling to regain his feet, to haul Neel with him.

But mad with terror, crying and babbling as if gripped by a nightmare from which he could not wake, Neel clung to Rowan like a drowning man, holding him down.

And the terrible creatures struck downward, blue mouths yawning wider, wide enough to swallow a man, teeth gleaming like long ice needles, teeth that sloped backward to strike deep, hold fast, drag into the freezing dark.

Ice creepers.

The creatures hissed, and the sound was like a knife cutting through fresh snow, and freezing breath gusted from their open mouths.

"No!" screamed Neel, and threw the lantern wildly. It flew uselessly sideways and smashed into the wall of the shed. Flames leaped upward.

Neel howled. His eyes rolled in panic. Then suddenly he was moving, flinging himself over Rowan's body, heedlessly crawling over it as though it were a log or a sack of grain, kicking back with his heavy boots, scrambling toward the fire.

The ice creepers turned their blunt, blind heads, following the movement.

And as Rowan crawled to his feet, one arm wrapped around his aching ribs, he saw only a white blur as one of the creatures struck down, and Neel was plucked, shrieking, into the air.

In seconds the beast had squirmed backward into the mist, there was a soft sound of sliding snow, and Neel was gone. Gone, into icy darkness. The creepers that remained turned back to Rowan.

Frantically he swept the torch from side to side, backing away, forcing himself to go slowly, feeling his way on the treacherous, slippery ground. The

beasts lunged, hissing, their breath cutting at him
like cold knives.

Rowan's limbs seemed to freeze. He staggered.
The flame wavered. Through the roaring in his ears
he heard Shaaran screaming, Bronden cursing
harshly, calling his name. Shaaran and Bronden had
reached the fence. They had seen . . .

"Stay back!" he heard himself shouting hoarsely.
"Get away!"

But already there were heavy steps behind him
and the sounds of panting and sobbing. Rowan felt
someone grabbing his arm. He caught a glimpse of
Bronden's wild-eyed face as she thrust him roughly
behind her.

Then Bronden was shielding him with her own
body. Bronden was facing the beasts, a flaming
torch held high, her sword gleaming in her other
hand. And Shaaran, sobbing and shaking, was
beside him, her frail arm around him, supporting
him, her own torch lifted so that it flamed beside
his.

"Back!" shouted Bronden. "Back!"

She took a giant step backward, and Rowan and
Shaaran stumbled back behind her. But the ice
creepers were following, their jaws gaping, their
heads striking down, down, down. . . . .

8 ∓ Facing the Truth

 Out of the corner of his eye, Rowan could see fire flickering where the lantern had fallen against the feed shed. The old wood had caught, and flames were licking upward.

"The fire!" he shouted. "Bronden! Move to the—"

Bronden heard and began to edge in the direction of the shed. Slowly, slowly . . .

Then Norris, panting and cursing, came stumbling out of the mist, a flaming torch in one hand, Lann's sword in the other.

Bronden's eyes slid toward him. It was just a glance, the matter of a split second. But it was fatal. For as she looked, her torch tilted slightly to the left, and like lightning a creeper struck, its terrible teeth fastening in her right side, just above her waist.

Bronden gave a groaning gasp. Her sword fell from her hand. Desperately she flailed in the creature's grip as it dragged her upward.

Rowan threw himself forward, catching her around the knees as her feet left the ground. Norris, shouting with horror, threw aside his torch and seized her left arm. But even their combined strength was not enough to hold Bronden back.

Wildly, Norris slashed at the beast's ghastly head with Lann's sword. The sword slid off the shining white hide with the sound of clanging metal. The beast seemed to shudder but did not let go.

It would never let go. It had struck Bronden only a glancing blow, but its teeth were embedded in the padding of her coat and had sunk into the flesh beneath.

Shaaran, white faced, was sweeping her torch from side to side, protecting them from the other beasts that writhed around them.

"Shaaran!" Norris roared. "Leave us! Run!"

Shaaran made no answer.

"Bronden's coat!" Rowan gasped. "Norris! Get her coat—off! Then hold her legs! Hold her!"

Norris seized the back of Bronden's coat and heaved. There was a tearing sound as seams ripped and fastenings burst. Rowan waited an agonizing moment while Norris took a firm grip on Bronden's legs. Then he thrust his torch straight at the beast's head.

The creeper jerked, hissing violently. Bronden gave a scream of anguish. And then the creeper was recoiling, the torn coat still flapping in its teeth, and Bronden was slumping to the ground, blood from her side sprinkling the snow.

The other ice creepers lunged forward in fury. Rowan, Shaaran, and Norris clung together over Bronden's body, their torches held high in aching arms, the flames wavering and small, holding the terrible creatures back.

They all knew they could not last. The creepers knew it, too. Their smooth, gleaming bodies arched and writhed. Their heads bobbed lower. They seemed to grin as their terrible mouths widened, hissing. . . .

Then Lann's defiant shout echoed through the mist, and the feed shed exploded in flames. Flames roared through the roof. Red-hot sparks and fragments of burning hay sprayed into the air. Waves of heat billowed over the snow.

The ice creepers reared back. There was a stealthy, slithering sound, like snow slipping from a roof. And the next moment—they were gone.

Hardly able to believe what had happened, that they were safe, Rowan, Shaaran, and Norris dragged Bronden toward the fire, their heads lowered to protect themselves from the sparks falling all about them.

The blessed heat enfolded them as they reached the gap in the fence. The snow beneath their feet melted and steamed. Lann was waiting for them, her wrinkled face black with ash, her teeth bared in a ferocious grin.

"That gave the devils pause!" she rasped.

Except for her stick, she was empty handed. She had given her sword to Norris. And Rowan knew that the torch she had carried to the field was in the burning shed. Lann, the most determined protector of the village stores, had thrown her torch into the precious hay. To speed the fire. To save their lives.

As if she felt his thoughts, Lann glanced at the inferno that the shed had become. Her grin of triumph faded, leaving her face gray and haggard. "There was no other way," she muttered.

"It does not matter now," Rowan replied. His voice sounded like the voice of a stranger, even to himself.

Lann looked at him searchingly for a moment. Then her lips tightened, and she bent to examine Bronden's side.

"Flesh has been torn away," she said, stripping off her own coat to lay it over Bronden. "A painful wound, but a strong woman like Bronden should not have been felled so completely by it. And there is too little blood for my liking. It is as though contact with the beast has chilled her to the bone. We must get her out of the cold without delay. Carry her between you. I will take the torches and lead the way."

Slowly, clumsily, Norris, Rowan, and Shaaran lifted Bronden from the ground. Her body hung limp between them, a dead weight.

They had only taken a few steps when Shaaran suddenly halted. "Oh . . . but what of the bukshah?" she cried. "We cannot leave them to—"

"Use your ears, girl!" Lann snapped. "Have you ever known the bukshah herd as silent as this? And use your eyes!"

She jabbed her stick at the ground. In the light of the fire still raging in the ruins of the shed, all could see the broad, trampled trail leading through the gap in the fence, and on into the mist and darkness.

"Star took the herd away long ago, Shaaran," Rowan said quietly as they began to move once more. "She must have waited till I left, then done what she knew was right. So when the creepers came, the field was empty of prey. Except for Neel."

Lann and Norris looked around at him, startled.

They had arrived too late to see what had happened to Neel.

"When Bronden and I reached the field, Neel . . . was there," Rowan said, his eyes fixed on the ground. "He had been hiding in the feed shed. For some reason he came out in the dead of night."

"To steal food from the storehouse, no doubt," said Lann grimly.

"Perhaps," Rowan said. He was reluctant to speak ill of Neel, though his bruised ribs still ached from the heedless kicks of the potter's boots. "In any case, he must have seen that the fence had been broken down while he slept. He went into the field to see if the bukshah had truly gone—"

"And found more than he bargained for," Norris finished grimly.

Shaaran gave a strangled sob.

"Neel was always too curious for his own good," Lann muttered. "Curious and weak minded, like his father before him." She shook her head. "Yet his father died peacefully in his bed, and Neel should have done the same—*would* have, no doubt, if this disaster had not befallen us."

She hunched her shoulders and pushed on through the snow. "It is unfortunate. Neel was never a merry soul, even as a child, but he could whistle to charm the birds from the trees. And his pots were as well crafted as anyone could wish."

The words were plain and dry, like Lann herself. But to Rowan they brought back vivid memories. The sound of whistling drifting from the pottery on sweet summer nights. The sight of Neel sitting at his potter's wheel, his wet, bony hands coaxing spinning lumps of clay into bowls, jugs, and beakers.

Neel had not been the most likable man in Rin. But he had been as much a part of it as the Teaching Tree or the House of Books. Now he was gone.

A vision of Neel's face as he had last seen it— white with frozen sweat, mad with terror—rose before Rowan's eyes. He wondered if he would ever forget it.

The forlorn little group trudged on in silence.

"Neel was weak minded, perhaps," Shaaran said in a low voice as at last they reached the village streets and began laboring toward the bakery. "But he was right all along. He warned us that this was the Cold Time come again. He warned us of the ice creepers. He warned us, and we would not listen, and he died because of it."

"He died because of his own folly, girl!" snapped Lann.

"And what of the other things he said, Shaaran?" Norris demanded. "Surely you do not believe that the Mountain is punishing the village because of us? Because of the silks?"

"I do not know what to believe," Shaaran whispered. "I only know that there must be a reason for all this. And if the reason is not what Neel claimed, what is it? When you and I came here, Norris, the village was full of life. Now it is all but dead. The people are gone. The bukshah are gone—"

"*We* are still here, Shaaran of the Silks," said Lann stoutly. She stopped at the bakery door and threw it wide so that Bronden could be carried inside.

Shaaran bit her lip. When she spoke again, her voice was unsteady. "We are here for now," she said. "But how long will it be before we, too, are gone? It grows colder every day. Monsters have come down from the Mountain, seeking prey. They have already invaded the fields. Perhaps soon they will be in the streets."

"Be still, Shaaran," growled Norris. "If they come we will defend ourselves. That is all."

They put Bronden down in front of the still-glowing fire.

"Bring blankets, Rowan!" Lann ordered, kneeling painfully beside the unconscious woman. "Also bandages and healing balm. Norris, feed the fire. And you, girl, make yourself useful by putting water on to boil. We have work to do here."

Shaaran went toward the kitchen, but at the doorway she turned. Two spots of vivid color burned high on her cheeks. She looked directly at Rowan.

"Lann refuses to discuss this," she said in a high voice. "And Norris turns away his head, pretending to be busy with the wood basket. But you know I am right, Rowan, and—and you know more than you are telling."

Her usually gentle eyes were snapping as the words tumbled out of her.

"What did Sheba say to you, Rowan? I know that it was more, far more, than you have admitted. I have seen it in your eyes all this long day. The time has come for you to tell the truth. And the time has come for us to face it, whatever it may be."

An icy hand seemed to grip Rowan's heart. A suspicion had entered his mind the moment he saw the broken fence and the tracks of the bukshah leading away into the darkness. Now suspicion became dread certainty.

When it is time, you will know it.

"Yes," he said huskily. He felt Lann's shocked, angry eyes upon him, heard Norris give a startled grunt.

"Sheba gave me a prophecy," he said. "The words were fearful, but I could not grasp their meaning. Perhaps I did not want to. Now, I think, I understand at least the first of them. As for the others . . . "

The room was still. The eyes of his companions were fixed on him. Rowan swallowed, stared into the fire, and slowly repeated the rhyme.

"The beasts are wiser than we know
And where they lead, four souls must go.
One to weep and one to fight,
One to dream and one for flight.
Four must make their sacrifice.
In the realm twixt fire and ice
The hunger will not be denied,
The hunger must be satisfied.
And in that blast of fiery breath
The quest unites both life and death."

For a long moment the silence in the room was broken only by the crackling of the fire. Finally Lann spoke.

"Sacrifice?" she whispered, her face stricken.

"The beasts . . . " Norris said. "The creepers . . . ?"

Rowan shook his head. "Not the ice creepers. The bukshah. They have been straying from their field for weeks. Always before I have brought them back. This time I know that I should not do so. Their feed is burned. There is nothing for them here. But they will lead me—to where I must go."

"The rhyme says *four* souls must follow, not just one." Lann was scowling. "But Bronden is injured, and I—am not able bodied."

Everyone in the room could see what this admission cost her. Her wrinkled face was set as though it were made of iron.

Norris drew himself up in his chair. "I will go with Rowan," he said.

Lann pursed her lips. "You cannot—"

"I can," Norris insisted. He turned to Rowan, who was shaking his head. "And do not think of creeping away alone, my friend," he said. "If you do, I will follow you. My place is beside you."

"And mine," Shaaran said, her voice trembling.

"No!" Rowan exclaimed sharply. "Norris, tell her—"

But Norris bent his head and kept silence.

Rowan stared at them hopelessly. He knew he could not fight this anymore.

"But still," said Lann. "That will only be three."

Dream pictures were vivid in Rowan's mind, like painted silks stirred by the breeze.

Three figures trudging through the snow, a fourth figure watching from a distance. Three figures huddling in a cave, a fourth shadow close by.

One to dream . . .

Rowan's skin prickled. "Three will be enough," he said.

"How can you know that?" asked Norris, eyeing him curiously.

Rowan hesitated, wishing he had held his tongue. *Learn what it is to be what I am.*

A vision of Sheba's grinning face loomed up at him. Sheba, hideous and cackling, brimming with spite, foam gathering at the corners of her mouth as she muttered over her evil-smelling fire. Sheba, feared and loathed by all.

The thought of her filled him with revulsion. The idea that people might think he was like her made his stomach churn. The gift of prophecy she had thrust on him was like an infection. He knew he had to hide it, keep the dreams secret. He would never admit to it and see Lann's lip curl, see Shaaran and Norris draw back from him in fascinated dread.

"Three—will *have* to be enough," he said at last.

"And where do you believe the beasts will lead you?" Lann demanded harshly.

Four must make their sacrifice.
In the realm twixt fire and ice . . .

Rowan wet his lips. "To the Mountain," he said. "I think we must go—to the Mountain."

9 The Carved Chest

 As soon as Bronden had been cared for, preparations for the journey were quickly made. Food, fuel, torches, ropes, and clothes were packed. Then there was nothing to do but wait. Even Rowan, worried that it would snow, covering the bukshah tracks, knew that they could not set out until it was light.

Lann, keeping watch over the still-unconscious Bronden, ordered them to sleep, but only Norris was able to obey her. With a calm Rowan envied, he flung himself down on his bed and was snoring in moments.

Shaaran moved to her own corner of the room, but when she was out of Lann's sight she quietly settled herself before the silk frame and took up her brushes once more.

Rowan lay unsleeping, every now and then getting up to check for falling snow.

At last the sky began to lighten. It had not snowed, but when Rowan slipped out the kitchen door he realized that the air was not warming as dawn approached. It was freezing cold—even colder than it had been the morning before.

The door creaked behind him. He jumped slightly and looked around. Lann was standing in the doorway, a lantern in her hand. Her lined face was shadowed with weariness from her long night's watch.

"It will soon be time for you to leave," she said, her breath making clouds of mist in the freezing air. "I must fetch some items from my home before then, and I would be glad of your help."

Rowan nodded, swallowing hard as they began to walk. For the first time he allowed himself to face the fact that Lann and Bronden would be alone after this morning. An old woman and a gravely injured one, with little food, and less hope, to sustain them.

"How is Bronden?" he asked.

"She has not stirred," Lann said grimly. "She is still cold to the touch, though she is beside the fire and wrapped in many blankets. The girl is watching her."

"Lann, I am sorry—" Rowan began. The old woman raised her hand to silence him.

"You are doing what you must do, Rowan of the Bukshah," she said. "And Bronden and I are also playing the hand fate has dealt us. There is no more to say."

They reached Lann's narrow cottage, and she led the way inside. The house was sparsely furnished and scrupulously tidy. It smelled of well-worn leather and sandalwood.

Lann looked around, her face expressionless. Absently she touched the back of the chair that stood by the empty hearth. There, Rowan guessed, she had spent her evenings in peace. Before this. All this . . .

"Because of Sheba's path, the people will reach the coast far sooner than we expected, Lann," he blurted out. "A rescue party will return with food and other supplies. Jonn promised."

"Indeed he did," Lann answered, still gazing about the room. "But as to what the rescue party will find when it arrives . . ."

Abruptly she shook her head and removed her hand from the chair. Rowan trailed after her as she hobbled to the tiny bedroom at the back of the house. She pointed with her stick at the iron bed.

"There is a wooden chest beneath the bed," she said. "Please pull it out."

Rowan bent to do her bidding. The chest was

heavy, and he could feel rich carving beneath his fingers as he dragged it into the open. He supposed it contained more blankets or perhaps bukshah-skin rugs.

Lann lowered her lantern. Soft light glowed on the chest's lid, illuminating a carved pattern of birds, beasts, and flowers.

"Why, it is beautiful!" Rowan exclaimed. Too late, he realized that Lann might be insulted by his obvious surprise. It was just that he had not expected her to own such a thing. Everything else in the house was so plain.

Lann did not seem annoyed, however. She herself was gazing at the chest with something like wonder.

"It is very fine," she agreed. "I have not seen it closely for a long time. For many years it has been too heavy for me to move into the light."

Stiffly she bent to touch the carving with the tips of her fingers. "It is fitting that you admire it, for it was made for me by Morgan, your father's father, as a wedding gift," she said.

This time Rowan's gasp of surprise made her smile slightly.

"Ah, yes," she murmured. "We were betrothed at one time, your grandfather and I."

She sighed. "Morgan was a fine-looking man. Your father looked very like him. Family resemblances are often very strong in Rin. As your father grew to manhood, I used to look at him and think, You could have been my son, had things happened differently."

My father, who died saving me from a fire, Rowan thought, and looked at Lann with new eyes.

Throughout his childhood he had known that most of the villagers thought that a puny, sickly boy was a poor exchange for a strong and well-liked man. He now understood that Lann must have felt even more bitter than the rest. She had hidden it well. Why was she telling him now?

"The village thought it would be a fine match, for both Morgan and I were heroes of battles against the Zebak," Lann continued, without raising her eyes. "But . . ." She shrugged. "But the marriage never took place."

"Why?" asked Rowan, then wondered how he could have dared ask such a question. He waited for Lann to rebuff him, but she did not. She answered, her voice halting as if the words were difficult to form.

"Morgan had a much younger brother, whose name was Joel," she said, staring down at the carved chest. "Joel had been born when his mother was long past the usual age of childbearing. By the time he was ten years old, both his parents were dead, and Morgan was his only guardian."

Her worn fingers traced the graceful lines of the carving—birds in flight, lizards crouching by tufts of grass, flowers twining.

"Joel was a frail, dark-haired child—dreamy and shy, frightened of his own shadow. He was of little use in the fields. He could not fight. The other children mocked him. The people despaired of him."

Rowan felt his face grow hot. Lann could have been describing his own childhood. And he could tell by her voice and her lowered eyes that she knew it only too well.

"Was Joel, too, a keeper of the bukshah?" he asked in a low voice.

"Yes. It was work he could do," Lann said. "As you know, that task is always—*was* always—thought of as too easy for anyone but the very young or those who were in some way wanting."

Her lips tightened. She seemed to be forcing herself to go on.

"I despised Joel," she said. "I thought him weak and cowardly. The strengths Morgan saw in him— his gentleness with all animals, his loving nature— meant nothing to me. It shamed me to be seen in his company. But Morgan would not abandon him. Morgan said that Joel must live with us until he was grown. We quarreled over it. Quarreled bitterly. Soon the whole village knew all was not well with us and guessed the reason. I did little to conceal it."

She sighed, her fingers rubbing, rubbing at the carving as if somehow she could smooth away the past.

"I was young," she said. "Young and angry. Jealous, too, I think, of Morgan's loyalty to his brother. We all paid the price for my pride."

Rowan stared at her, speechless. Never had Lann spoken of her feelings to him—or to anyone else, as far as he knew.

"What happened?" he asked. The story had given him a dark, sinking feeling. He understood now why no one had ever told him of it before, and he did not want to hear its end. But he knew that the old woman wanted to tell it.

"Joel was killed," Lann said flatly. "He feared heights, but he climbed a tree to hide from some children who were taunting him because he had come between Morgan and me. His pursuers discovered him in the tree. They threw stones as he tried to climb higher. The next moment, he was falling. Perhaps a stone hit him. Perhaps he merely slipped. Or perhaps he just—let go. . . ."

Her voice trailed off, and the little room seemed to dim with the shadows of the old tragedy. Rowan's eyes burned as he thought of the frail boy, shamed and desperate, hounded to his death because . . .

Because he was like me, Rowan thought. A throw-
back to an older time, when our weak and our
strong, our brave and our gentle, our artists and our
warriors lived together as one people. Before the
Zebak separated us and brought the strong, brave
ones to this land, leaving the gentler ones behind.
Whenever Lann looks at me, she sees Joel again.
And she remembers . . .

"Joel fell from the great tree—the tree beneath
which we of Rin marry and farewell our dead,"
Lann murmured. "It was a strange twist of fate that
it should have been so, for when Joel died beneath
that tree's shade, my hopes of marriage with
Morgan died with him."

She was still staring at the chest, still smoothing
its carving with her work-worn fingers.

"Morgan came to me that night and gave me
this chest," she went on in a voice so low that
Rowan had to strain to hear her. "He said Joel had
drawn the pattern from which he had carved it. It
was to have been their joint gift to me. He said
no more, uttered no word of anger or blame, but
I knew his feelings for me had changed. I could
see it in his eyes. I released him from our
betrothal."

Slowly she straightened and met Rowan's eyes.
"Years later he wed Else, your grandmother. I was

glad that he had found happiness at last. Or told myself so."

"And you . . . ?" Rowan asked.

"I never found another to match Morgan, so I remained alone," Lann said, with some return of her old briskness. "No doubt it was for the best. I have always been too fond of my own way to share my life with another."

"I am sorry," Rowan mumbled, not knowing what to say.

"Ah, well. It was all long, long ago," Lann said. "And what is done is done."

For a long moment she was silent, then she firmed her lips determinedly and fixed Rowan with her familiar steely gaze.

"Open the chest, if you please," she said.

The metal clasp was stiff, but at last Rowan managed to loosen it. Carefully he opened the lid.

Somehow he was disappointed to find what he had expected. The chest was filled with bukshah-skin rugs, loosely rolled.

Lann gave a gasping sigh. She bent and gathered one of the rugs into her arms. Then she shook it out and let it hang loose.

And Rowan saw that it was not a rug at all, but a long, hooded cloak. A bukshah-skin cloak, made of whole hide, with the ragged wool on the outside and the leather, still amazingly soft and supple, within.

He had seen its kind before, in paintings and drawings in the House of Books.

And he had seen it in his dream of the Mountain.

"I have four of these," Lann said. "They are Rin warrior cloaks—the last remaining in the village, for the young prefer woven garments now, it seems. One is mine, two belonged to my parents, and one was Morgan's, given to me by Else when he died. They have seen much. And they will warm you as nothing else will. You and your companions."

She pulled three more cloaks from the chest, shaking them out carefully, piling them into Rowan's arms.

Rowan could not speak. There was a roaring in his ears. But Lann was still speaking. He forced himself to attend to her.

"You and I have not always agreed, Rowan of the Bukshah," she said. "I have found fault with you, as once I found fault with Joel. You, no doubt, have thought me harsh and set in my ways. But over these past years, I have come to see that though we are very different, you and I, we are not unalike in all the ways that matter."

Seeing Rowan's stunned expression, she lifted her chin. Her weathered face warmed as she looked away from him.

"I do not pretend to understand this . . . this thing that has been asked of you," she said stiffly. "If it is as it seems, it goes against all I have ever believed of our lives, and this land."

She paused. She was breathing heavily, as though she was struggling to control some deep emotion. Rowan waited.

"I am old, and my time in this world will soon be over," Lann said at last. "What I have to give my people has already been given. You are a different matter. It is very bitter to me that the weakness of my body prevents me from facing this ordeal in your place."

Rowan knew better than to insult her with useless thanks. He told her, instead, the truth.

"You could not have taken my place, Lann, even if you had the strength," he said bluntly. "You could only have accompanied me, as Shaaran and Norris seem fated to do. Sheba told me that only I could do what must be done."

Lann took a sharp breath. "Only you?" she rasped. "The one who climbed the Mountain and faced the Dragon to make the stream flow again? The one who has forged bonds of trust with the Maris and the Travelers? Who gave us knowledge of our past, and saved us from the attack of the Zebak?"

She turned away. "What evil would require our best as sacrifice?"

The hunger must be satisfied.

Rowan felt a cold shuddering begin deep within him.

Without warning, in this narrow house filled with the everyday objects and shadowed memories of an old woman's lifetime, the fear he had kept in check for so long escaped and threatened to overwhelm him.

His heart pounded. He was gripped with the urge to flee.

How easy it would be! To drop the cloaks on the floor and go back to the bakery. To snatch up the bag he had packed and run, along Sheba's clear, blackened path, through the hills and away.

In a day he could be far from here. The way would be hard and long, but at last he would reach the coast. If his own people would not take him in, if they turned from him in disgust, he could find a home with the Maris or the Travelers. On the coast, he could make a new life. He would be safe—

The medallion hanging around his neck seemed to throb. He clutched it, intending to tear it from him.

But as his fingers touched the warm metal, the words of Sheba's rhyme began echoing, echoing in his mind. And with the words came a vision.

Rin, locked in a silent, frozen dream. Ice creepers twisting and sliding through the orchard trees and the still, white streets. The Mountain brooding above it, breathing cold malice over the land and into the sky. And the deadly chill spreading, spreading, never ceasing. Till the plains where the Travelers once roamed were deserts of misty white and waves no longer crashed on the Maris shore, for the sea itself had frozen and grown still.

And Rowan knew that this was the future. The future if he ran. The future if he failed.

Rowan . . . ?

The voice of the Keeper of the Crystal whispered in Rowan's mind, soft as foaming water. The vision was so strong, so clear and compelling, that the Keeper was sharing it. Deep in his rainbow cavern, far away in Maris, the Keeper, too, was gazing at those snowy wastes, that frozen sea.

"Rowan? Rowan!"

This voice was real. The hand shaking his arm was real also. Slowly Rowan turned to meet Lann's anxious eyes. He wondered how long he had been standing motionless, transfixed by something she could not see, listening to something she could not hear.

The frantic urge to flee had vanished, leaving sour shame in its place.

"Let us go back to the others," he said. "It is nearly time to go."

10 ∾ Four Souls

Rowan, Shaaran, and Norris left the village as the Dragon on the Mountain roared at dawn. Their path was clearly marked. The bukshah tracks lay on the snow like a broad, dappled ribbon, following the line of the buried stream and disappearing into the trees that clustered at the foot of the Mountain.

All three of the companions wore bukshah-skin cloaks. As Lann had promised, the cloaks were very warm. They were surprisingly comfortable, too, though they almost brushed the ground. Lann had been forced to shorten two of them with her knife so that Rowan and Shaaran could walk without stumbling.

Norris carried Lann's sword and a long staff to lean on as he limped along. Shaaran carried the box of silks, which she had refused to leave behind.

"I am the keeper of the silks," she had said stubbornly when Norris and Lann railed at her for her foolishness. "They must be with me. I feel it."

They passed the mill standing tall and silent, its great wheel stuck fast in a bed of ice. On they went, and on, resting now and then but speaking little. Rowan knew that the sun must be climbing higher behind its thick veil of cloud, but the light did not brighten, and the air did not warm.

As they neared the Mountain, the trees grew more numerous and the bukshah path narrowed to wind between them. The trees stood like drooping sentinels, their dark branches bowed down with snow. The muffled stream gurgled eerily. The freezing air seemed hard to breathe. Ahead the Mountain loomed, huge and menacing.

Rowan fixed his eyes to the ground, trying to think of nothing. The medallion grew warm. Unwillingly he raised his hand to it.

Learn what it is to be what I am.

He heard the sound of splashing water and looked up. Through the trees he saw . . . saw three figures in bukshah-skin cloaks, kneeling beside a small pool at the foot of a sheer cliff. As he watched, one figure straightened, screwing the cap on a dripping water flask. Then the figure stilled and suddenly looked over its shoulder, straight at Rowan.

Like looking in a mirror. But the dark, anxious eyes were unfocused, searching—

"Ah, this is where the stream begins!"

It was Norris's voice. Rowan blinked. The figures ahead shimmered and disappeared. Now only the cliff remained. Water gushed from a black hole near the cliff's base, splashing into a deep, round pool that was only partly iced over.

Norris pulled his water flask from his belt and went to fill it. Rowan followed but remained standing as Shaaran knelt beside her brother to fill her own flask.

"What is wrong, Rowan?" Norris demanded, staring up at him. "You look as if you have seen a ghost!"

It would be madness not to fill my flask, just to prove that the vision was not a picture of the future, Rowan thought. There is no fighting this. I was foolish to try.

Wearily he dropped to his knees and bent to let his flask fill to the brim. As he straightened he could not resist glancing back at the place where he had stood only minutes before. Of course he saw nothing—nothing but a mass of black trunks, dark, snow-laden branches, and the tracks winding back toward the village.

Then his eye caught a flicker of color in the sky

above the trees—a flash of bright yellow, startling against the gray. The flash came again. Something was swooping toward them, moving fast. With a sharp cry of warning Rowan jumped up, reaching for his knife.

"What is it?" cried Shaaran in terror.

But already the vivid yellow shape was billowing above them. Then it was folding in on itself and sinking downward. And Rowan gasped with astonishment to see, hanging beneath it, a lithe figure swathed in a bukshah-skin cloak.

It was Zeel of the Travelers.

Rowan stared, stunned, as Zeel's soft boots hit the ground, her yellow silk kite collapsing behind her. Shaaran and Norris were exclaiming, but he could not speak.

"You are surprised to see me, Rowan!" Zeel laughed, gathering up the trailing silk and draping it over her shoulder. "Why, you gape like a Maris fish! But surely you knew I would come?"

Rowan found his voice at last. "No," he choked. "I never dreamed of it. Why . . . ? How . . . ?"

Zeel moved quickly to his side and clasped his hand. "The Travelers are camped just outside Maris," she said. "The Keeper of the Crystal summoned Ogden at dawn and told him of the vision he had shared with you. Ogden hastened back to our camp with the news and I left at once, to join you in your quest."

One for flight . . .

The words seemed to flame in Rowan's mind. He had thought they meant that he, Shaaran, or Norris would flee from danger at last. But he had been wrong, quite wrong—as he had been wrong to think that his dream self was to be the fourth member of this ill-fated party.

The fourth member stood before him now. Ogden's adopted daughter Zeel, Rowan's friend, straight and strong, full of life.

What evil would require our best as sacrifice? The memory of Lann's voice, shaking with anger, seemed to roar in Rowan's ears.

He felt Zeel's hand tighten on his.

"I flew over your people marching toward the coast along a strange black road, Rowan," she said. "I found your village deserted except for the old warrior Lann and the woman Bronden, deep in a frozen sleep. I learned that you, Shaaran, and Norris had gone alone to the Mountain, following the tracks of the bukshah. Rowan, why did you not call me before this?"

"There is—great peril . . . " Rowan began haltingly.

"I know that!" Zeel cried. "Why else am I here?"

"But I thought that Travelers could not survive the

cold of the inland winter!" exclaimed Norris. "And I have heard that for Travelers the Mountain is forbidden!" His face was furrowed with anxiety. He knew Zeel from the adventure in the land of the Zebak, and very much admired her.

"That is true." Zeel grinned, her white teeth dazzling in her brown face. "But have you forgotten, Norris? I am not Traveler born. I was a Zebak infant—a foundling washed up on this land's shore and adopted by Ogden long ago. I can do what other Travelers cannot. I can climb the Mountain if I must. And I can survive bitter cold, though"—she shivered, drawing the cloak more closely about her—"though never have I felt such cold as this. I confess I am glad of the strange garment your old Lann gave me."

Thoughtfully she smoothed the shaggy fur. "Lann has changed. Once it would have enraged her to think that a Traveler—let alone a Zebak—might wear a Rin warrior cloak. But she made me take it. She said it had been waiting for me."

"That is because Sheba's rhyme said four souls would follow the beasts," Rowan muttered. "But Zeel, the rhyme speaks also of death, and sacrifice."

Zeel nodded, and the last traces of her smile disappeared. "I know," she said. "The rhyme passed from your mind to the Keeper's with the vision. As soon as I heard it, I knew that I was destined to join you and to share your fate, whatever it might be."

"No!" The word burst from Rowan's lips like a groan of pain.

Zeel drew herself up. "The land is under threat. Why should Rin alone make sacrifice, if sacrifice there must be? I am here of my own free will, with the Keeper's thanks and Ogden's blessing, to represent the Maris people and the Travelers. I rejoice that by an accident of birth I was the only choice that could be made. I rejoice that my kite could bring me to you quickly."

Her pale blue eyes swept across Shaaran's fearful face, and Norris's excited one, then returned to Rowan.

"We are four quarters of a whole," she said. "Each of us has a part to play in this. Each of us is needed. We do not yet understand how or why. But we will find out soon enough. And then . . . what will be, will be."

The bukshah tracks continued around the base of the Mountain until the cliffs of the eastern face gave way to tumbled masses of barren, snow-covered rocks on the southern side.

And there the trail turned sharply inward and began to climb.

The companions halted, and a great silence enfolded them. Nothing moved. Not a breath of wind stirred the freezing air. The Mountain brooded above them, waiting.

"At last!" exclaimed Norris, rubbing his hands with relish. "Here the real test begins!"

Rowan glanced at him, wondering. Norris's eyes held no trace of fear. His head was high, his strong shoulders thrown back. His mouth was set with grim determination.

So Lann must have looked, preparing to do battle with the Zebak, long ago, Rowan thought. Norris is a true child of Rin. Strong. Fearless. A warrior.

Then Rowan felt a movement beside him and looked around. Shaaran, too, was staring at the Mountain. But her delicate face was filled with dread. Desperately she clung to the box of silks, pressing it hard against her body to still her trembling hands.

Rowan thought of the pictures within the box—the paintings full of color, life, and movement. He thought of Shaaran's hand deftly moving the slim brush over silk, creating truth and beauty as her ancestors had done for centuries.

And with a jolt he remembered that Shaaran was also a true child of the people of Rin. Not the Rin people as they were now, but as they had been centuries ago, in the land of the Zebak, when artists and warriors lived side by side, and gentleness was valued as highly as strength. Before the strong ones were taken away.

And suddenly, in the terrible, waiting stillness, it was as though the parts of a puzzle fell into place.

Four souls . . .

Four quarters of a whole . . .

Shaaran and Norris, who were living proof of the story the silks told.

He, Rowan, who had brought them to the valley.

And Zeel, representing all those who had helped him do it.

We have offended the Mountain . . .

An icy finger touched his heart.

The bukshah had picked their way between the rocks, making a narrow path that twisted and turned. With Rowan leading, Norris and Shaaran following him, and Zeel bringing up the rear, the companions followed the trail.

It was hard and awkward work, especially for Shaaran and for Norris, who was badly hampered by his injured leg. But neither of them asked for rest, and neither Rowan nor Zeel suggested it. The light was slowly fading, and all of them felt in their bones that this brutal maze was no place to be when dusk fell. So grimly they pushed on, always climbing and always moving west.

Gradually the rocks grew larger, rising high above them, blocking their view of the way ahead. And at last the path was only a narrow, zigzagging track lying deep between sheer black cliffs, and there was no way to go but forward or back.

They crept along in the gloom. The way grew narrower till the sky was just a slit of dull light far above them. The rocky walls that hemmed them in were marked by strange, long scratches at shoulder height. Rowan realized at last that these must have been made by the horns of the bukshah as the beasts pushed their way along the narrow path.

The medallion at his throat seemed to throb in time with his heart. His pack dragged at his shoulders, heavier by the moment.

"I do not like this." Zeel's voice echoed eerily. "What if we are being drawn into a trap? If something comes for us here, there will be no escape."

Norris mumbled agreement.

But Rowan barely heard them. He had turned a corner, and suddenly his whole attention was riveted on something only he could see. Not far ahead, the passage ended in a rocky archway. Beyond the archway, strange blue light glowed. And within the light, something was moving.

Rowan froze, squinting at the wavering shape. Then his heart seemed to leap into his throat as he saw the swirl of first one long, heavy cloak, then another, and realized what the shape was.

Cloaked figures were walking ahead, walking in the blue light. They were one behind the other, heads bowed, pressed so closely together that at first they had seemed one creature. They were moving forward, very fast.

And they were afraid. Rowan could feel their fear. *Make haste! Stay close. Do not look . . .*

His skin prickling, hardly aware of what he was doing, Rowan opened his mouth to cry out. But before he could make a sound, the figures had vanished.

Rowan slumped against the cliff face on one side of the pathway, jamming his shoulder against the icy rock to keep himself upright. His knees were weak. His heart was still thudding with fear. The archway gaped ahead, blue light glowing. He could hear Shaaran, Norris, and Zeel's exclamations as they caught up with him and they, too, saw the light. But he could not speak.

Clearly there was something fearful on the other side of the archway. He dug his gloved fingers into the hard rock to still their shaking.

"What is it?" Shaaran cried. "Rowan, what is that place? What must we do?"

And suddenly the medallion was scorching hot. Wincing with pain, Rowan clutched at it, trying to lift it away from his skin. But to his amazement it would not move. It seemed fastened where it lay, and the more he pulled at it, the more it clung to him and the hotter it became.

He saw his companions turning to him in alarm as he cried out. He saw them reaching for him as he slid to his knees, tearing at his throat. But they could do nothing for him, nothing. For now it was as if the thing on his neck was sinking into his flesh. It was burning, burning, and his throat was filling with what felt like red-hot coals, filling to bursting till he was choking on fire.

He tried to scream, but as his dry lips gaped open there was no scream. Instead he felt the choking lumps of fire rise from his throat into his mouth and spill out into the freezing air. Even in his agony he was stunned to realize that they were not burning coals at all, but words—words that burst from him in a hoarse, grating voice he barely recognized as his own.

"Within this vale the blind are wise.
Horrors lurk behind your eyes.
The cure is water from a well
Where hate and anger do not dwell."

When the last word had been uttered, Rowan pitched forward into the snow, and knew no more.

11 ∽ The Blind Are Wise

Rowan came to himself slowly and painfully. His head was throbbing. He felt dizzy and sick. He could feel a soft hand patting his cheek and could hear voices calling him, but he did not want to open his eyes. He wanted nothing more than to sleep, sleep forever.

But the voices would not let him rest.

"Rowan, wake!" That was Zeel's voice, urgent and commanding. "We cannot stay here!"

"He is bewitched!" That was Norris, almost shouting. "Those words were not his! And that voice . . . that was not—"

"Rowan, open your eyes." A gentler voice, Shaaran's voice, close to his ear. "Rowan, the bukshah need you. We must follow them. Remember?"

The bukshah . . .

Memory swept through Rowan's mind, and with a shuddering jolt he was wide awake. His eyes flew open. He clutched at his throat. Beneath his clothing the skin was smooth and undamaged, the medallion dangling harmlessly from its cord. He struggled to his feet, helped by six eager hands.

"What happened?" demanded Norris, clearly shaken by what he had just seen and heard. "You began raving, words that had no meaning, Rowan, and your eyes rolled back . . . " He broke off with a shudder.

"The medallion . . . " Rowan's voice was choked and husky. He cleared his throat and tried again. "Shaaran asked a question, and the medallion gave me the words to answer it. I cannot explain—"

"Do not try," Zeel said sharply. "We have our advice and our warning. There is danger beyond the archway. We know what we must do to protect ourselves against it. That is all that matters for now. We must move on, and quickly. The afternoon is waning."

Rowan nodded and, without saying anything more, began trudging unsteadily toward the glimmering blue light. Shaaran, her eyes dark with fear, crept after him.

Norris followed, continually glancing back at Zeel, searching her watchful face for answers to his confusion. At last, as the archway yawned ahead, filling their view, he could keep silence no longer.

"Why do you say we know what to do?" he burst out. "We know nothing!"

"Did you not listen, Norris?" Zeel snapped. "The rhyme told us that in the vale the blind are wise. Surely that means that what we do not see will not harm us."

"What?" Norris exclaimed. "Are we to walk into the unknown with our eyes closed?"

"We cannot do that," Rowan said without turning around. "But we must make ourselves as blind as we can. Once we enter the blue light, we must put our heads down and follow the path, looking neither right nor left—at least until we reach this mysterious well that is a place of safety."

As he spoke, he was remembering the vision he had seen, remembering the cloaked figures walking quickly, close together, their bent heads hooded.

He shuddered as again he felt their fear.

Make haste! Stay close. Do not look . . .

The archway was before him now. He stopped, steadying himself against the rock. The blue light seemed to swirl before his eyes like colored mist. And now he could see the gleam of ice. The place beyond the arch was studded with great, twisted ice columns that rose from the earth like trees!

The ground was bare of snow. So the vale was

covered. It was a cave—or perhaps a vast tunnel through the rock of the Mountain.

"It seems to me that only a fool would march through an evil place without keeping watch," Norris was muttering. "What if the rhyme is a snare?"

"It is not a snare!" Zeel flashed. "And *you* are a fool, Norris, to suggest it."

Norris flushed dark red and squared his heavy shoulders. "Perhaps I *am* a fool," he mumbled. "My grandfather always thought I was, I know, because I had no talent for painting, and no ear for music, and because I relished fighting. But I saved his life in the land of the Zebak, many times, by being wary, by knowing an enemy when I saw one, and by being ready to fight, as he and Shaaran were not."

"That is true," Shaaran said in a low voice. "Without Norris we would never have survived."

Zeel frowned. "I beg your pardon, Norris," she said awkwardly. "I spoke without thinking. You are right to be wary. You have not had as much experience of these rhymes of prophecy as Rowan and I have had. But, believe me, they can be trusted."

Norris met her level gaze and nodded slowly. "Very well," he said. "But if we are to walk blind, let us at least stay close together so that we cannot be separated."

"That would be wise," Zeel agreed. She moved

closer to him and put her hand on his shoulder. Blushing even more deeply, this time with satisfaction, Norris took hold of Shaaran's shoulder. Shaaran took hold of Rowan's.

"Heads down," Rowan said, and heard Zeel murmur a blessing. He took a deep breath and moved through the archway, his companions shuffling behind him.

The blue light closed in around them. And with it came the fear. Fear seeped into Rowan's mind like freezing water, chilling his blood, pooling in his heart. His skin prickled with awareness that they were not alone, that something here was aware of them, something filled with malice.

He felt Shaaran's hand tighten on his shoulder, heard her gasping breaths, and knew that she, too, was gripped by terror.

"Keep your head down," he whispered. But even as he forced the words from his dry lips, his urge to raise his own eyes was becoming almost overwhelming.

Spires of ice loomed at the edges of his vision like blue shadows. The bukshah's hoofs had made only faint marks on the hard ground, so that their narrow, winding trail was almost invisible. Many times Rowan was forced to hesitate before cautiously moving on.

Then the trail seemed to disappear altogether. A pillar of ice lay directly ahead, and Rowan could not tell if he should turn left or right.

He stood paralyzed, desperately searching the misty ground. His forehead was beaded with freezing sweat. He was terrified of making the wrong decision. The thought of becoming lost, wandering aimlessly in this fearful icy maze, filled him with dread.

He felt Shaaran press against his back as if she was being crowded from behind.

"I have lost sight of the trail," he called. "Wait—"

He broke off as Norris cursed ferociously and Zeel gave a long, drawn-out hiss.

Rowan felt a spurt of anger. Did they not know how hard this was? Let *them* try to lead, then.

"I am doing my best!" he shouted. "Be patient!"

There was a roar of baffled rage, then a weird, high cry, and suddenly Shaaran was pushed into Rowan's back so violently that he was almost thrown off his feet. Rowan shouted, staggering, fighting to stay upright as Shaaran clutched at him blindly.

Behind them someone fell heavily, crashing onto the hard ground. Rowan felt his cloak pulled and twisted, and he groaned aloud as he realized that Shaaran had turned to look over her shoulder.

Shaaran screamed piercingly, screamed his name. *Within this vale the blind are wise.*

The words rang in Rowan's ears, but he could no longer listen.

He swung around, thrusting the shrieking girl aside and partly behind him.

And, in horror, he saw that they had walked into a trap. Two figures were grappling on the ground. They were fighting savagely, rolling between twisted columns of ice. Blue mist swirled about them, veiling them, so Rowan could not see whether it was Zeel or Norris who had been attacked. But he could see the bright blade of a dagger. He could see spatters of scarlet blood on the ice.

Fumbling for his knife, he shrugged his pack from his shoulders and sprang forward, shouting. One of the struggling figures threw the other heavily aside and leaped up to face him.

The breath caught in Rowan's throat and he drew back, his heart pounding with shock. Snarling ferociously before him was a Zebak guard, her face smeared with blood, the tattooed black line that marked all her people running like a frowning furrow down the center of her forehead.

The Zebak raised her dagger and sprang at him. Instinctively Rowan blocked her strike, seizing the wrist of her dagger hand, holding the weapon back.

Her weight threw him back against an ice pillar, which shattered like glass. His own knife fell from his hand and spun away.

They rolled, shards of ice splintering beneath them. He could feel the Zebak's hot breath on his face. He could feel her hatred. Her dagger gleamed above him, its blood-smeared point aimed at his throat. His hands and wrists were strong from his work with bukshah—they were his only strength—but already they were trembling with the strain. For how long could he hold the dagger back? How long . . . ?

In the background, someone was screaming. Shaaran. Shaaran was screaming frantically for Zeel. Why did Zeel not answer? Why did she not come to help him?

And suddenly Rowan knew. Zeel did not come because she was dead. As, no doubt, was Norris. This fiend had killed them both.

And that had been the Zebak plan. To pick the four off one by one as they shuffled blindly through the mist. To ensure that they would never reach their goal, never fulfill the prophecy.

And why? Rowan's mind was working like lightning. Why? Because the Zebak wanted this land, the land they had failed to conquer, to be doomed. They wanted its people punished for daring to defy them.

Scarlet rage blazed through him. His hands tightened on the Zebak's wrists, and with a strength he had not known he possessed he heaved her away from him, smashing her dagger hand against the jagged edge of the shattered pillar.

She shrieked with pain and rage. The dagger spun away. Rowan dived for it, seized it. . . .

And heard a strange sound.

He looked up and saw, rising directly in front of him, something dark and hideous. It was a squat, twisted tree. Its thick, stubby branches, tipped with clumps of dull purple leaves, were heaving and thrashing. Its fat white roots were already snaking hungrily toward him.

Rowan gasped, rigid with horror. This was a tree of Unrin—a tree with a taste for human flesh, a tree like those that had long ago smothered the Valley of Gold.

He and Zeel had fought them together in the Pit of Unrin, had nearly died in their loathsome clutches. But the Mountain was the killer trees' natural habitat, and this one was here, reaching out for him, greedy for him. . . .

Shuddering with disgust, Rowan made himself move. He scrambled backward, trying to keep his feet clear of those hungry, snakelike roots.

His cloak was tangling around his legs, hampering

him as he tried to get up. He could hear Shaaran shrieking, sobbing wildly, and with a surge of panic he realized that she was running toward him. Her cries were growing louder. He could hear her steps, very near.

"No, Shaaran! Keep away!" he roared, slashing at the roots as they struck at him.

His mind was racing. By now the Zebak must be clambering to her feet, her rage fanned to white heat by the pain of her injuries.

She had lost her dagger, but she would attack with her bare hands if she had to, injured or not. And she was strong, very strong. She would do anything to complete the task she had been given. She would snap Shaaran's slender neck like a twig. She would wrest her dagger from Rowan at last and kill him, too.

But . . . Rowan's heart gave a great leap. The killer tree! The Zebak would have no way of knowing how dangerous it was. If he could lure her into its clutches . . .

He risked a glance behind him to see if his way was clear. And his heart seemed to stop as he saw, rearing above him, a twisting white shape with gaping, blue-lined jaws and wicked, needle-sharp teeth.

12 ⟡ The Well

Dagger raised, Rowan stared up at the ice
creeper, waiting for death. He was beyond
terror now, beyond sorrow. His mind was
wiped clean of every feeling but one: pure hatred.
If he was to die, if all was lost, he would take as
many of his enemies with him as he could.

He saw the Zebak crouched behind the beast, a
shard of razor-sharp ice clutched in her bleeding
hand. He felt a killer-tree root seize his ankle, gripping it like an iron band.

So. Let them all fight over him, and kill one
another in the battle.

He braced himself against the grip of the killer
tree. He laughed at the Zebak, taunting her, daring
her to come closer. Then he looked up at the ice
creeper once more. Above the hideous jaws the

creature's head was gleaming, as though some vile liquid was oozing from its skin. Rowan's face twisted with loathing.

The creature gave a strange, hissing gasp. It bent closer, its eyeless head nodding closer to him, closer . . .

Rowan tightened his grip on the dagger, preparing to strike. Then—astonishingly, he felt a splash of something warm on his upturned face.

And instantly the ice creeper coiled, shrank, vanished. In its place was Shaaran—Shaaran, bending over him, the box of silks clutched in her arms, tears streaming down her cheeks.

Rowan gaped at her, thunderstruck. The dagger fell from his hand. Then his heart seemed to leap into his throat as he saw a shadow rise behind the weeping girl—a shadow wielding a deadly blade of ice.

The Zebak!

"Beware!" he shouted. He grabbed Shaaran's arms and pulled her down, down and to one side. The plunging blade missed her by a hair, and her attacker pitched forward, stumbling over their rolling bodies and falling heavily to the ground.

And only then did Rowan see that the attacker was . . . Zeel! He blinked, unbelieving. But there was no mistake.

There was no Zebak warrior. There never had been. It was Zeel who was crawling to her knees before him, one hand bleeding, the other fumbling on the ground for a weapon.

Stunned by shock, horror, and joy, Rowan gave a choked cry. At the same moment, Zeel's seeking hand closed on his knife, which had been lying half hidden behind an ice column. She staggered to her feet. Her glazed eyes focused on him. Her face creased into lines of loathing.

"Die, ishkin!" she hissed, hurling herself forward.

"Zeel, no!" Rowan shouted. But even as the words left his lips, even as he jerked back and the knife slashed clumsily through the place where he had been, he understood.

Horrors lurk behind your eyes.

Frantically he cursed himself for his stupidity, for not thinking more carefully about the words of the rhyme.

The line said *behind* your eyes, not before them! He raged at himself. And what is behind your eyes? Your mind, you fool! Your mind! *That* is the treachery of this place. It shows you the enemies that live in your memory. Zeel is not seeing you as you are! When she looks at you she sees an ishkin, a monster from the land of the Zebak. Just as you saw *her* as a Zebak guard and Shaaran as an ice creeper. Enemies you hate as well as fear . . .

With a start, he glanced down at his imprisoned ankle. Instead of a killer-tree root, he now saw Norris's gloved hand holding him in an iron grip, Norris's arm outstretched stiffly, Norris lying face down on the ground, still as death.

"Rowan!" Shaaran screamed. Rowan looked up just in time to see her throw herself toward him as Zeel struck again.

And the next instant the knife aimed at his heart had plunged into the wooden box Shaaran held before him like a shield. The side of the box splintered. The precious rolls of silk began sliding out, spilling and rolling on the hard ground.

Shaaran gave an agonized cry. Zeel seized her and threw her violently to the ground.

"So, you would feed me to the ishkin, would you, guard?" she hissed at Shaaran. "You would like to see me skinned and dragged under the earth, like my friends? Well, no doubt you will have your wish. But you are coming with me, alive or dead!" Her bloodstained hands moved to Shaaran's neck and tightened.

"No, Zeel, no!" Shaaran sobbed, clawing feebly at the strangling fingers.

Rowan struggled to pull Zeel back, to break her hold. It was useless. His mind was roaring with horror. Must he use Zeel's own dagger to save Shaaran? Was it to come to that?

"What—what is wrong with her?" Shaaran choked.

"She thinks you are a Zebak guard," Rowan said. "As I thought *she* was, until—"

He broke off.

Until what? What had broken the illusion? Why had he been cured so suddenly, so completely? What had . . . ?

The final words of the rhyme were suddenly ringing in his ears.

The cure is water from a well
Where hate and anger do not dwell.

Understanding struck him like a bolt of lightning. "Shaaran!" he shouted. "Wipe your eyes, then touch her face! Now! Make haste!"

It was typical of Shaaran that she did not question him, did not hesitate. She lifted her hands from her throat, smeared the tears from her eyes, then placed her fingers on Zeel's cheeks.

And instantly Zeel blinked and lurched back, her face showing her shock. Her hands fell from Shaaran's neck, and she stared at them as if they did not belong to her.

"Zeel!" shouted Rowan, filled with joy.

She turned to him blankly. Then, as memory flooded through her, she looked down at Shaaran lying gasping amid a tangle of silk.

"What . . . have I done?" she breathed, aghast.

"Do not grieve," Shaaran managed to say, crawling to her knees. "It was not your fault, Zeel. Truly it was not."

"You did nothing that I did not do, Zeel," Rowan said. "And Norris. Shaaran was the only one of us who—"

A low groan made him turn in alarm.

Norris was waking. He lifted his head and opened his eyes. He looked full into Rowan's face. His eyes darkened, and he bared his teeth. His hand tightened on Rowan's ankle.

With a cry Shaaran began crawling painfully toward her brother.

Swiftly Rowan reached out, swept his fingers over the girl's wet cheeks, and smoothed the tears onto Norris's frowning brow. Norris shuddered all over. Then the frown lines vanished from his face, leaving it smooth, bewildered, and almost childlike.

"I—I was dreaming," he mumbled. "Shaaran, you are alive! And Rowan! But I thought—"

Abruptly his face became alert, and he began

struggling to rise, blood flowing freely from a terrible knife wound in his side.

"Norris, do not move!" Shaaran cried. But already
Norris had gained his feet and was looking around
wildly.

"There is a Zebak guard here!" he hissed. "She
killed Zeel and took her place, somewhere on the
trail. I blame myself. I heard nothing! I only knew
when I turned to speak to Zeel, after we stopped.
The fiend attacked me—we fought. . . . "

He tried to straighten, groaned, and clasped his
side. "And there is a fighting grach here, too—
huge! A killer! I had hold of it—trying to keep it
back from you—but now I cannot see it! Rowan,
Shaaran, get behind me. Where is my sword? My
sword!"

Rowan saw the sword lying on the ground. He
picked it up and thrust it into Norris's hand. "Here
it is, but you do not need it, Norris," he said. "There
is no one for you to fight. No guard, no grach." He
sighed. "Just as there was no ice creeper, no killer
tree . . . "

"No ishkin," Zeel added soberly, limping over to
join them. "They were illusions, Norris. We almost
killed one another, fighting our memories."

Norris swayed, shaking his head in confusion.

"But I saw nothing!" Shaaran said huskily, one

hand at her bruised throat. "I saw only you—all of you—attacking one another. And your faces . . . " A shadow seemed to cross her own face, and she shuddered.

"You saw nothing because you have no enemies to see, Shaaran," Rowan said.

Shaaran almost laughed. "Why, that is ridiculous!" she cried. "I have more fears than all the rest of you put together!"

"You *fear* many things, but you *hate* nothing," Rowan said. "There is not a person or a creature you would willingly destroy, even to save yourself. Is that not true?"

Shaaran stared at him, her face coloring faintly as though, somehow, she was ashamed.

"Grandfather was the same," Norris mumbled. "And our mother and father, too. Protecting them was an almost hopeless task."

"That I can well imagine," Zeel said fervently. "But it seems that this time the situation was reversed."

Norris looked bewildered.

He saw nothing of what happened, Rowan thought. He still does not understand.

"Shaaran saved us all," he told Norris. "Remember the last lines of the rhyme? The well where hate and anger do not dwell was not a real well at all, but Shaaran's overflowing heart. And the healing water was her tears."

"*One to weep*," said Zeel.

Shaaran's blush deepened.

Norris scowled. "Then why did the rhyme not say so plainly?" he growled. "Why should we be tricked and puzzled by a riddle?"

"There is an old Traveler saying that life itself is a riddle we must all solve for ourselves," said Zeel. She spoke lightly, but her eyes were thoughtful.

Shaaran had begun collecting the scattered rolls of silk. "I cannot see the bukshah tracks at all now," she said nervously. "I fear we are lost."

But Rowan could see his pack still lying where he had dropped it, not too far away.

"All is well!" he exclaimed, pointing. "That is where I left the path!"

"Thank the heavens." Zeel sighed with relief. "Then let us bind our wounds, mend the box of silks somehow, and leave this accursed place as fast as we can. Its very air sickens me."

Within the hour the companions were slowly threading their way through the columns of ice once more, this time with Zeel in the lead. It had not taken long for her keen eyes to pick up the trail that Rowan had been unable to find.

All four of them were hurt, but Norris was in the worst state. His injured leg had been further damaged in the fight, and the wound in his side was deep and painful.

But was his suffering the only reason for his heavy silence? Rowan wondered. Or did the real trouble lie somewhere within?

For Norris's face was like thunder. He did not join the chorus of feeble cheers that greeted the sight of another rocky archway ahead—an archway through which a blur of dull gray could be seen. He did not look up as the companions struggled at last out of the vale of horrors and into the open air.

This does not bode well, Rowan thought. And as he looked about him and recognized the bleak, steep, snow-covered slope that lay beyond the archway, his heart sank.

A bitter wind swept around them. The light was dim. The bukshah tracks showed dark on the snow, climbing upward until they were lost among tumbled rocks. Beyond the rocks was a wall of towering black cliffs. Above the cliffs there was nothing to be seen but swirling mist.

Three figures, trudging upward in single file.

This was the place of his dream. The first dream of all.

But the dream will not come true, Rowan told

himself. It *cannot* come true. Norris and Shaaran and I are not alone. Zeel is with us.

He realized that Zeel was speaking to him. "We must find shelter, and soon," she was murmuring. "A place where we can light a fire."

Three figures huddled in fear around a fire.

"The cave . . . " Rowan mumbled.

"Cave?" Zeel exclaimed. "What cave?"

Rowan shook his head to clear it. "I only meant . . . there . . . there must be a cave, surely, in those cliffs above," he stammered.

Zeel considered him with her head on one side. "Why are you so certain?" she asked.

Rowan hesitated. He could see that Zeel suspected he knew more than he was telling. In one way he longed to confide in her. But he had not admitted to his terrible dreams before, so how could he do so now, in this bleak place, with Shaaran and Norris hovering on the edge of despair?

Zeel shook her head impatiently. "Keep your secrets, then!" she snapped. "But if you *know* there is a cave, Rowan, it is madness not to tell me. We are in danger! Where are we to go? How are we to hide?"

And instantly the medallion grew hot. In horror Rowan snatched at it, consumed by the memory of that burning pain, that terrifying feeling of being taken over by something other than himself.

"Oh, Rowan! I did not mean to . . . oh, I am sorry!" Zeel's cry rang in his ears. "Rowan, do not fight it! Let it . . . "

Her voice faded away.

Do not fight it.

Rowan resisted the urge to pull the burning medallion away from his skin. Instead he pressed it closer. The heat began deep in his throat, scorching and swelling, but he forced himself not to choke. And so the strange words flowed from him, not easily, but not agonizingly, either, out into the icy air.

"Refuge waits on high ahead.
Climb the ladder of the dead.
Hide within the rocky walls.
Be still while icy darkness falls."

13 ∽ The Climb

As the last word of the rhyme left his lips, Rowan fell to his knees in the snow, sick and dizzy. Slowly the world seemed to steady, and he looked up. Norris was staring at him dully. Shaaran was staring, too, her hand pressed to her mouth. And Zeel . . .

Zeel was unfolding her kite.

"No, Zeel!" Rowan cried in panic. He struggled to his feet, staggering as fresh waves of dizziness swept over him.

Zeel glanced at him. "I did not mean to put you through that pain, Rowan, but at least I can make it worthwhile," she said. "The rhyme spoke of rocky walls. There must indeed be a cave up ahead. I will search for it from the air while you begin to climb."

"No!" Rowan argued desperately. "One of your hands is injured, Zeel. And it is too dangerous to fly here. If the wind changes you will be dashed against the cliffs!"

Zeel raised her head. "You forget," she said quietly. "I am a Travelers' Forerunner. My task in life is to fly ahead of the tribe in all weathers, seeking shelter, watching for danger. My skill can aid us now. I would not risk the extra weight of a passenger, but alone I can do it, one handed if I must."

She lifted the kite so that the yellow silk billowed above her. "I will see you again, Rowan," she said.

Rowan recognized the words. They were used by Travelers farewelling one another in perilous times.

"I will see you again," he replied. Zeel grinned at him, turned her face to the wind, and was swept up and away.

For a moment Rowan watched the kite swooping above them, a splash of brightness against a background of white, black, and gray. Then he turned back to Shaaran and Norris.

They were both still looking after Zeel, Shaaran with fearful wonder, Norris in despair. The young man was swaying where he stood, his face lined with strain, his shoulders bowed.

Rowan's heart sank. "We should light torches before we move on," he said. "We have a long climb ahead, and at any moment . . . " His voice trailed off as he met Shaaran's terrified eyes. He did not have to remind her of what might even now be sliding toward them beneath the snow.

Norris said nothing. Even when Rowan thrust a flaming torch into his hand, he did not speak, just turned and began to limp away, following the bukshah tracks.

Shaaran glanced at Rowan, her eyes filled with anxiety.

"Let him go," Rowan said. "Just follow." Dread weighed him down. He knew what was going to happen next, but he was powerless to prevent it.

Learn what it is to be what I am.

In single file the three trudged upward. In Rowan's mind was a vivid picture of what they must look like. The tall, limping figure in the lead, the small, fragile figure next, clutching a long wooden box, he himself last of all. . . .

Unable to resist the temptation, he turned and looked behind him. He saw nothing but snowy wastes, black rock, and the archway, glimmering blue.

"Rowan, what is it?"

Shaaran had stopped and was staring at him in alarm.

Rowan shrugged, determined to say nothing. He saw that Norris had also stopped and turned. Norris's eyes were haunted, but he did not speak.

This at least is not the same as it was in the dream, Rowan thought with a flash of hope. By holding my tongue, I have changed things. Perhaps . . .

"Let us move on," Shaaran urged. "Soon it will be dark."

Norris's lips stretched into a ghastly smile. "What does that matter?" he said suddenly. "Whether we stop here or higher on the Mountain, whether it is night or day, we are doomed."

His stick and his torch fell from his hands and he crumpled to the ground.

Shaaran ran to him and began pulling his arms, calling his name. He merely turned his face away from her and burrowed deeper into the snow, like a child unwilling to rise from a cozy bed.

"Rowan, help me!" Shaaran screamed.

Rowan snatched up the fallen torch and forced himself to think.

I saw us all in the cave together, he reminded himself. I know that somehow Norris can survive this—that we can all survive it. But I also know that pleading with him and reasoning with him will not make him move. There must be another way.

But what other way? He and Shaaran did not have the strength to carry Norris, or even to drag him more than a short distance up this steep slope.

"Get up, Norris, oh, please!" Shaaran was crying.

She was kneeling by her brother now, half buried in snow herself.

"Let me sleep," Norris mumbled. "This is the end."

This is the end.

Rowan saw Shaaran cover her mouth with her hand to muffle a cry of despair.

This was where his dream had ended. What now?

He threw himself down beside Norris. "It is not the end, unless you make it so, my friend," he said evenly.

Norris heaved a deep, shuddering sigh. Then he rolled onto his back and looked up at Rowan.

"It *is* the end," he said. "We all had our part to play in this quest. One to weep, one to fight, one to dream, one for flight. Is that not so?"

Rowan nodded and waited.

"Shaaran is the one to weep," Norris said, staring up at the darkening sky. "Her tears saved us all in the vale of horrors. You are the one to dream, Rowan, for you wear the medallion and say the rhymes. Zeel is the one for flight, as we have just seen. And I . . ."

His voice broke, and he closed his eyes.

"Go on!" Rowan urged, fighting back the guilt that had flooded through him at the mention of dreaming. "And you—you are the one to fight?"

"Of course!" Norris burst out, his eyes flying

open. "I thought I was destined to be your protector. I was so sure of it that I did not even try to prevent Shaaran coming on this journey. I thought I
was going to save you both."

Shaaran gave a choked sob. Norris's eyes slid in
her direction, then immediately slid away.

"I was so proud of the part I was fated to play," he
muttered. "I, who was always my grandfather's
despair, was going to prove at last that I was a hero,
not a fool."

He gave a snort of bitter laughter.

"Norris—" Rowan began. But Norris was not listening.

"When the time for fighting came, how joyfully I
rushed into the attack!" he went on, his face twisted
with pain and shame. "But then—then I found that
I had not been fighting enemies at all, but the
friends I had sworn to defend. I had been a heedless
fool, yet again. And now I am nothing but a
wounded, useless burden."

"Zeel and I also fell victim to the visions!" Rowan
exclaimed. "You cannot blame yourself for what
happened."

"I can, for I was the one who turned. I was the one
who began it all, playing the great guard and protector," said Norris. "And now our quest is done. I
realized it when I saw Zeel launch her kite.

Dreaming, weeping, fighting, and flight. All four parts have now been played."

Rowan's stomach turned over.

"And my part," Norris continued, his voice sinking lower, "my part, far from saving us, has been to leave us weak and helpless, easy prey for whatever fate the Mountain has in store. I have been nothing but a pawn in a wicked game."

His eyes were burning with bitter tears. "Leave me. I do not want to live through what is to come. The evil thing that brought us to this place has triumphed."

He turned back into the snow, covering his head with his arms and drawing up his knees to his chest.

"Norris!" shouted Rowan, shaking him. "Even if you are right—even if we have been led by some evil force into a trap—we cannot just lie down and die!"

But this time Norris did not stir.

There was a strange, high call from somewhere above. Zeel! Rowan clambered to his feet, looked up. The yellow kite was hovering near the cliff face, one side dipping slightly as though pointing to a place below.

He felt a stab of hope. Zeel had found the cave. All they needed to do was reach it, and there would be warmth, rest, some sort of safety.

But Norris lay like a log in the snow, binding

them to this bleak and dangerous hillside. Norris, of all people! He who was so admired by all in Rin for his strength and courage.

Rowan felt anger rise within him. He knew it was unworthy and unfair, but for an instant he let it possess him. If Lann could see Norris now! Or Bronden! What would they do?

And suddenly he knew. Lann and Bronden would treat Norris as they would expect to be treated themselves. They would know by instinct what would pierce the shell of despair that had enclosed him, for he was like them.

Rowan took a deep breath and steeled himself.

"Get up!" he said, and kicked Norris's shoulder contemptuously.

Shaaran shrieked.

Rowan ignored her and kicked again.

Norris opened his eyes. "Leave me be," he groaned.

"Coward!" Rowan sneered. "You coward!"

"Rowan, how *could* you?" cried Shaaran. "He is in agony."

But Norris's dull eyes had kindled, and his face had darkened with anger. "You call *me* a coward?" he growled.

Rowan turned away. No doubt it looked to Norris as if he was turning away in disgust. Norris could not see that his tormentor had his fingers crossed and was holding his breath.

But Shaaran could. Her shocked eyes widened in understanding, and she fell silent.

Norris moved. Clumsily he felt for his stick. When he had it in his hand, he crawled painfully to his feet. Caked snow fell from his clothes in a heavy shower. He snatched his torch from Rowan's hand. "I will show you who is a coward," he snarled. "Keep up with me if you can!"

He staggered away, following the trail.

Shaaran and Rowan began toiling after him. No doubt he is cursing me, Rowan thought. But at least he is alive.

Alive for now. Rowan pushed the unwelcome thought away and doggedly pressed on.

The climb was long and hard. It grew colder and darker, and the wind was bitter, stinging their faces, blowing the smoke from their torches into their eyes. The way grew steeper and more winding as they neared the cliff face. Vast boulders hulked around them. The churned snow beneath their feet was icy, frozen hard into jagged lumps, and slippery as glass.

Zeel circled above their heads, watching for signs of danger—danger writhing beneath the snow, hidden in the mist that now swirled among the rocks.

At last the cliffs rose huge and dim before them.

The bukshah tracks straggled off to their left, but Zeel swooped toward the right, and the three on the ground followed, floundering through deep snow. Soon the kite was hovering like a great yellow butterfly over a place where the top two-thirds of the cliff face bulged out over the rest, shadowing a dark, narrow opening in the rock.

Rowan at once recognized the opening as the cave of his dream, though without Zeel's help he would surely have passed it by. Seen from the outside, the narrow, ragged triangle seemed a mere crack in the rock. And it was not at the base of the cliff face as he had expected, but a third of the way up, just below the overhang.

Refuge waits on high ahead.

The rhyme had spoken the literal truth. The cave was a high refuge indeed. How were they to reach it? The cliff face below it was straight and smooth, impossible to climb.

Rowan quickened his pace, passing Shaaran and Norris, almost running. When he was directly below the cave, he flattened himself against the cliff face and lifted his hand as high as he could. The tips of his fingers fell short of the opening by at least a body length.

Climb the ladder of the dead.

"You must stand on my shoulders."

Startled, Rowan turned. Norris had come up beside him, his face drawn with pain and exhaustion.

"You first, Rowan, so that you can help Shaaran from above," Norris said. "Zeel can follow her."

"Norris, you are not fit—" Rowan began. But Norris shook his head.

"To reach the cave you must climb the ladder of the dead, so the rhyme said," he muttered. "And what am I but a dead man?"

Shaaran, still struggling toward them, heard his last words and exclaimed in horror. Norris did not turn to her. His eyes were fixed on Rowan.

"I cannot reach up to that gap, and the three of you together could not lift me," he said. "But I can be of service to you. And then perhaps—perhaps you, Zeel, and Shaaran might have a chance of surviving this. It would mean so much to me to think it might be so. Rowan, I am begging you!"

Rowan could not deny him. Quickly he nodded, and with a muffled groan, Norris bent his back. Ignoring Shaaran's cry of distress, Rowan climbed onto the broad shoulders. Then, as Norris slowly straightened, he lifted his hands and grasped the base of the cave mouth.

His muscles strained as he hauled himself upward. His boots scrabbled uselessly on the smooth rock of the cliff face. But the thought of falling back onto the ground, of having caused Norris pain for nothing, gave strength to his arms. In a few moments he was sprawled, panting, on the cave floor.

The cave was gloomy but shallow. He could see well enough to tell that nothing lurked in its shadowy corners. Quickly he squirmed around so that he was facing outward again and slid forward so that his head and shoulders protruded from the cave mouth.

Norris was bent double. Shaaran was crouched beside him, sobbing.

"Shaaran!" Rowan called, stretching out his arms to her.

But she was shaking her head. "He is in agony!" she cried. "I cannot do it!"

Rowan heard a sharp cry of warning from above. He looked up. The yellow kite was wheeling and plunging. Zeel was signaling wildly. He looked down again, and his heart thudded as he saw that the thick snow farther along the cliff face was moving, rising into a smooth, white drift.

Something was rushing toward Shaaran and Norris along the base of the cliff, snaking through the snow like an eel through water.

"Ice creeper!" Rowan yelled. "Shaaran! Norris! Beware!"

14 ∽ The Cave

 Norris straightened. Gritting his teeth, he seized Shaaran around the waist and with a groan swung her up, up with such tremendous force that Rowan was able to catch her around the shoulders and pull her into the cave.

They tumbled backward onto the sandy floor. Shaaran was screaming. Rowan picked himself up and scrambled back to the entrance.

Zeel was nowhere to be seen. She must have flown up to the top of the cliff and landed there, Rowan thought dazedly. She must have feared that the ice creeper would snatch her out of the air. But Norris . . .

Norris had his back to the cliff wall. The wound in his side had been torn open when he lifted Shaaran and was again bleeding freely. He was holding all three torches before him like a shield.

"Norris!" Rowan shouted, pushing himself forward and stretching out his arms. "Take my hands!"

Norris did not even look up. "Get back!" he bellowed. "You cannot lift me. Protect yourselves. Light a fire at the cave mouth. Make haste! I will hold the thing back as long as I can, but—"

The snow at his feet bulged, then the icy surface burst open and a hideous blind head reared up, mouth agape. Norris did not flinch. He thrust the torches forward. The creeper hissed, recoiled, prepared to strike again.

Rowan tore new torches from his pack and began trying to light them. His hands were shaking, and he cursed himself for his clumsiness.

Norris was shouting, jabbing with the torches. The beast was lashing in fury, its blue-shadowed maw gaping as it struck and struck again. Then it jerked as a yellow flash swept down from the cliff top and soared past its head in a flurry of heat and flame.

It was Zeel—Zeel, clinging to the kite with her good hand and brandishing a burning torch in the other. She had landed on the cliff top, certainly, but she had stayed there only long enough to coax the torch alight.

The ice creeper hissed and struck, catching the

edge of the yellow silk in its teeth. The silk ripped
with a high, terrible sound. The kite shuddered,
tipped sideways, began slowly to flutter downward.
The creeper reared and twisted toward it, ready to
strike again.

Norris saw his chance and took it. With a bellow he
launched himself forward, pushing the three bunched
torches straight into the beast's unprotected body.

There was a ghastly sizzling sound and a sour, hot
smell. Dark blue mist gushed in a hissing roar from
the beast's gaping mouth. For a moment the great
body seemed to tremble in the air. Then, as Norris
stumbled hurriedly out of its way, the creeper collapsed against the cliff face and lay still.

Norris stared with glazed eyes at the heap of
flabby coils that reached almost to the cave
mouth. He did not turn his head as Zeel came up
beside him, the sad, torn fragments of her precious
kite draped over her shoulder. But when she took
his arm he did not argue, and he allowed her to
support him as they approached the creature's
body.

Zeel touched it with her foot. Its skin was already
dulling and wrinkling slightly, and its flesh dented
under her boot.

"You killed it," she said with respect.

"But it was only a small burn, on such a large

body." Norris shook his head. "How could the creature die of it?"

"Heat must be like poison to it," said Zeel. "Like
poison in its blood. Ah, how you went for it,
Norris! Like a man possessed!"

"You gave me the chance I needed," he mumbled.

She shrugged. "I did what I could," she said. "But
it was your strength that saved us all."

He made a small, choked sound, and she glanced
up at him. His eyes were strangely bright, and the
taut muscles around his mouth had suddenly
relaxed, leaving his face smooth and peaceful.

What did I say to make him look so? she thought.
I only spoke the truth.

She puzzled over it briefly, then put it out of her
mind, as she had put her grief for her kite aside, to
concentrate on practical matters. Norris was staggering where he stood, and his clothes were soaked
with blood. She took a firmer hold on his arm.

"Come," she said. "You have given us our ladder.
Our ladder of the dead. Now we must climb it."

Together, with Rowan and Shaaran urging them
on, the pair crawled upward, using the lifeless
white thing as a ladder. The flabby coils slipped
and oozed with every step. Zeel's jaw was set and
her eyes were dark with horror. Norris was shaking
all over.

In moments they had reached the cave and were clambering inside. As soon as he had clasped their hands in welcome, Rowan set about lighting a fire. He knew that Shaaran would care for Norris. He knew that Zeel would want to be left in peace to mourn her kite in her own way. His task now was to make the cave safe—as safe as it could be—for the long night ahead.

As darkness deepened outside the cave, Rowan, Zeel, and Shaaran boiled a little water for tea. Then they toasted bread, which they ate first with melted cheese and then with some of the honey and dried fruits Zeel had brought with her.

The fire and the warm food and drink brought comfort to their minds as well as to their bodies. Even Norris seemed to revive a little after a time and was able to sit up, wrapped in blankets and leaning against the wall of the cave.

By unspoken agreement they did not speak of the past day or of the future, though there was much to be said. Instead they talked of small things—the sweet, fresh taste of the honey, past meals they had enjoyed.

Rowan talked of the salty, fishy food of the Maris. Shaaran and Norris spoke of the vegetables and fruits they had grown in the land of the Zebak.

Zeel told of the Travelers' bees, carried from place to place as the tribe followed the blooming of flowers in season.

Then her voice trailed away, and Rowan suspected she was remembering that a time could be coming when there would be no more flowers, or bees, or even Travelers in the land. When there would be nothing but the cold, barren whiteness of an endless winter.

He moved restlessly, trying to put the thought from his own mind. "We had better try to sleep," he said. "I will keep the first watch."

"I will keep the second," said Zeel quickly, before Norris could speak. "Do not fail to wake me when it is time."

Soon all was quiet. The cave floor was hard, but Norris, Zeel, and Shaaran were exhausted, and even their pain and fears could not keep them awake once they were curled up in their blankets.

Rowan kept watch as the long hours passed, sitting upright by the fire, watching the dancing flames. Occasionally he added a stick to keep the fire bright, but every time he did so, he felt a pang of fear.

The bundle of sticks they had carried with them was growing smaller by the hour. And if more creepers came, if he, Zeel, Norris, and Shaaran were besieged, trapped in the cave by dozens of the creatures . . . what would happen?

They had food, and they had water. But these would not save them if they had no fuel.

The fire would go out. The last of the torches would burn away. Then there would be nothing to stop the creepers from plucking them out of the cave one by one, like lizards snatching baby birds from a nest.

Hide within the rocky walls.
Be still while icy darkness falls.

Icy darkness . . .

Rowan shivered. Was this cave to be the end of the journey? Was this small hole in a freezing wall the place where they were all to die?

His heart was like a block of ice. His whole body felt numb. And then, in the silence, he heard faint sounds above his head.

His skin crawled. He listened. The sounds came again, chilling and unmistakable. Something was writhing and scrabbling above them, on the overhang.

The sounds grew louder. Chunks of snow began to fall from the edge of the overhang, plunging past the cave entrance to the ground.

Zeel sat up, instantly alert. Norris and Shaaran stirred, and their eyes flew open.

"It began not long ago," Rowan whispered. "There was only one at first, I think. But now there are many."

Zeel gritted her teeth. Shaaran began to tremble. Norris's face looked as if it had been carved out of stone. In all their minds, Rowan knew, was the terrifying picture of a twisting mass of white, snake-like bodies, blue-shadowed jaws, blind heads jabbing, jabbing at the rock, seeking entrance.

He added another stick to the fire. There was nothing else he could do.

"The fire will keep us safe," Zeel said. But she did not sound sure.

Rowan searched for something to talk about—anything to mask the terrible sounds.

"Tell us of our people on Sheba's trail, Zeel," he said. "Were they well?"

"Well enough," said Zeel, following his lead determinedly. "I did not go down to them, for I was intent on reaching you and did not wish to risk losing the wind. But they were marching along at good speed, intent on their purpose and looking straight ahead, as Rin folk do."

Despite herself, she half smiled. "All but Allun, whose Traveler ways have still not quite deserted him," she added. "I think he may have seen me, for he raised his arm. But I had passed in an instant, and I am not certain."

"And what of Lann and Bronden?" asked Shaaran, rousing herself to keep the conversation going, though her lips were stiff with fear. "How do they fare?"

"Lann has things well in hand," Zeel said. "She has encircled the bakery with all the old, useless wood she can find. She plans to dash the wood with oil and light it if needs be, to protect Bronden and herself from—"

She broke off, annoyed with herself for having reminded her companions of the danger that threatened them. For a moment they all became aware once more of the sounds above them.

The stealthy, rasping noises were louder now and seemed closer. It was as if every moment more and more ice creepers were slithering through the snow that smothered the overhang. As if a squirming mass of cold, white bodies was scraping now on the rock itself.

Zeel's eye fell on the box of silks Shaaran held in her lap. "Shaaran, let me see some of the silks again, I beg you," she said, raising her voice.

Rowan's heart lurched. So far everything had been different from the scene in his dream. But it seemed there was no escape from what was to come. Zeel was asking the very question that he himself had sworn not to utter.

"Ogden has talked of little else but the silks ever since he first saw them in your village in the summer," Zeel went on. "And I believe he thinks of them even more often than he speaks. It is strange."

She leaned forward to feed the fire, not noticing the sudden stillness of her companions. Rowan exchanged glances with Shaaran and Norris. He knew that they were sharing his thoughts.

Could it be that Ogden of the Travelers had sensed danger in the silks? Danger for the land? Now Rowan came to think of it, he had certainly studied the silks carefully, and left the village rather hastily thereafter.

He said nothing to me of any fears, but perhaps he wanted time to consider, Rowan thought. If so, he waited too long. But would we of Rin have listened to him, even if he had spoken? The people were so happy to learn a little of their past. They would not have welcomed a Traveler's warning.

He dragged his attention back to Zeel. She had warmed to her subject now and was speaking rapidly, staring into the fire. It was clear that Lann had said nothing to her of Neel the potter's fearful warning or his attempt to burn the silks. Zeel had no idea that every word she spoke fueled her companions' feeling of dread.

"It is puzzling," she said. "Over and over again Ogden has praised the skill with which the silks were made and the timelessness of this way of keeping history. But there is no doubt that there is something about them he finds . . . disturbing. Once, speaking of them, he said, almost to himself, 'What should I do? Speak out, tell what I suspect, or leave well alone?' But when I asked him what he meant, he turned away and would say no more."

She sighed. "It is a mystery. I resolved that when I had the chance I would try to solve it. Could I see the silks?"

Breathing fast, unable to refuse, Shaaran fumbled with the clasp of the wooden box. The box looked very battered. Its splintered side had been roughly lined with part of a blanket to keep the silks inside secure. Carefully Shaaran opened the lid.

No, Shaaran, thought Rowan. But already the girl was pulling rolls of silk from the box. She loosened one roll and spread it out. Rowan felt a chill run down his spine. It was the silk she had painted in the bakery.

The colors were brighter than the colors of the silk in his dream, but otherwise the painting was very much the same, hideously the same. Rowan stared at the well-remembered shapes of black, white, blue, and gray. He stared at the long line of people trekking away through snow-covered hills along a burned black path. He stared at the buk-shah, neatly fenced in their snowy field.

Then he turned his eyes with dread to the Mountain. During that last long night before they set out, Shaaran had not only finished the painting but added to it. Writhing from the mist of the Mountain were hundreds of hideous, snakelike shapes, with gaping, blue-lined jaws and teeth like shards of ice.

Zeel drew breath sharply and turned her face away. Norris gave a low groan.

"Oh, I am sorry!" Shaaran babbled, rolling up the silk with trembling hands. "I had to paint the truth. But I did not mean to show you this . . . "

Then suddenly there was a deep, low growling from the rock, and it was as if the world fell in, with a crashing wave of sound. Rowan pitched forward, clapping his hands to his ears.

Dimly he heard Zeel shouting, Shaaran scream-ing, and Norris cursing.

The fire went out. Then all was cold, and black-ness.

15🙰 Shadows

 The bukshah were walking in single file up a narrow stairway cut into rock. They did not look as Rowan remembered them. Their heads were high. Their horns were sharp and white. Their thick coats seemed to glow. Their hoofs were gleaming gold in the sunlight.

Rowan was climbing the stairway after them, following the prints of the golden hoofs. He was filled with dread. His legs were aching, but he knew he could not stop. There was no choice now. There was no turning back.

We must follow the beasts. . . .

Unwillingly Rowan raised his eyes. At the top of the stairs gaped a dark, steaming mouth, huge in the midst of rock that was seamed and pitted like an ancient face.

Hunger . . .

His eyes were blurred. The steps gleamed, dazzling, climbing up, up . . .

Dreaming. I am dreaming. . . .

Rowan woke, his mouth dry, his heart pounding. He opened his eyes but saw only blackness. For a single terrible moment he thought he had lost his sight. Then he heard Norris, Shaaran, and Zeel calling to one another and to him. He remembered what he had felt and heard just before he lost consciousness. And the words of the rhyme echoed in his mind, taunting him.

Hide within the rocky walls.
Be still while icy darkness falls.

Frantically he cursed himself for a fool. The last words of the rhyme had told him what was going to happen—told him in plain words, though he had failed to understand.

The overhanging cliff top, that great shelf of rock burdened with snow and squirming with ice creepers, had broken away and fallen. Snow and rubble had piled up against the cliff face. The cave mouth was blocked.

Rowan felt sweat break out on his brow. They were trapped. Hidden within rocky walls indeed.

Hidden forever. The dark seemed to press in upon him.

Blindly he felt for his flint and pulled a torch from his pack. As the torch flared, he caught a glimpse of Shaaran huddled against a wall, Zeel kneeling with her head in her hands, and Norris crouched by the cave mouth, holding his walking staff. The narrow triangle of the entrance gleamed white with snow.

Norris swung around, grimacing with pain as the movement pulled at his wound. "Put that out!" he roared. "The flame will eat the air we breathe, and there is little enough in here as it is!"

Hurriedly Rowan did as he was bid, shamed that in his panic he had not thought of this himself.

He heard Norris grunt with effort, then the thrusting, crunching sound of the staff plunging into the snow. The sounds came twice more. Then, suddenly, Norris gave a shout of triumph and Rowan felt a small draft of cool air on his face.

"I am through!" Norris called. "We are in luck! The blockage is mainly snow, I think—and snow that is not even as thick as my staff is long."

He began jabbing at the snow again. Soon a patch of dim light glimmered in the inky darkness, and the draft of cold, fresh air grew stronger.

"The creepers," whispered Shaaran. "They will be waiting."

"I would rather face a hundred ice creepers than remain in this tomb," Zeel said. "But it is safe to light torches now, so please do so, Shaaran, while Rowan and I help Norris clear the way. Then at least we can make a fight of it."

But the torches Shaaran hastily lit were flickering low by the time Norris, Zeel and Rowan had made a gap wide enough to crawl through. And when at last the four cautiously squeezed one by one onto the great pile of rock and snow that now sloped down to the ground from the cave entrance, the only ice creepers to be seen were dead.

A sulky dawn was breaking, and dull red stained the sky. The companions stumbled down to ground level, slipping on heaped snow and treading upon the remains of dozens of creepers lying crushed and withered beneath huge, broken chunks of rock.

When they looked about them, they saw that it was not only the overhang above their cave that had collapsed, but a long portion of the black cliff face. The giant boulders that once had clustered at the foot of the cliff farther toward the west were now invisible beneath a jumble of tumbled snow, rocks, and dead trees. And everywhere were the partly covered bodies of ice creepers, mangled and gray.

So many . . .

Rowan shook his head. It was as if someone had whispered in his ear. But that could not be so, for he could hear his companions talking to one another not far away.

"These dead creepers must be just a few of all those who were here. Think how many more must have escaped," Norris was muttering. "Why, there must have been hundreds of them moving in on us."

"How did so many know where to find us?" Shaaran asked.

"I think they must sense our warmth," Zeel said. "But whatever the case, it is fortunate that we did not camp in the shelter of one of those boulders, as I thought we might. We would have been killed, certainly, if not by the creepers, then by the collapse of the cliff. It was only because we were hiding inside the cave that we were spared."

No one will be spared. . . . Nothing will survive. . . . Cold, so cold . . . And there are so many . . . so many. . . .

The words hissed through Rowan's mind. Then there was a flicker at the edge of his vision, and he saw that all around him there were shadows, wavering shadows with gaunt, starved faces and hollow eyes. And with horror he recognized, beneath the lines of suffering, features he knew. The features of Jonn, of Bronden, of Timon, of his mother . . .

A deep shuddering began within him. He felt hot,

then freezing cold. His mind seethed with whispers, hissing and echoing, twisting and mingling,
sliding one upon the other.

So many . . . too many . . . What have we done?

Rowan pressed his hands to his ears, squeezed his
burning eyes tightly shut. But it was no use. The
shadows pressed about him. He could still hear the
whispers, still see the familiar faces, hideously
changed. His mother's hair was gray as ash. Her
eyes were red with weeping.

*We knew too much, and too little. We have been wrong . . .
so wrong . . . Now the Mountain makes us pay . . .*

Someone touched his hand. "Rowan!" a soft voice
called.

The shadows faded. The whispers died away.
Rowan swayed.

"You are not well, Rowan," he heard Shaaran say.
"You are faint." Her voice rose. "Norris! Zeel!"

Rowan heard exclamations, felt strong arms lower
him gently to the ground. He sat with his head
bowed, and gradually the waves of sick dizziness
grew less and the world came back into focus. Zeel
and Norris were on either side of him. Shaaran was
kneeling in front of him, offering him water.

Gratefully he drank. His head was throbbing. The
dim light hurt his eyes.

"I am sorry," he mumbled. "I could not help—"

"Was it another rhyme? Tell us!" Norris urged.

"No—not a rhyme." Rowan swallowed. "I saw . . . "
He broke off with a shiver.

Zeel had been watching him keenly.

"I think there is something you must tell us,
Rowan," she said. "I have thought so for some time.
But this is not the time or place. We are too
exposed to danger here. Can you walk?"

Rowan managed to nod, and she helped him to
his feet.

"We will take it slowly," she said. "I will help you."

"But the bukshah tracks were covered when the
cliff fell." Norris frowned, looking around him. "We
have lost the trail."

Zeel shook her head. "I saw the trail from the air
last night," she said. "It followed the cliff west, then
entered a grove of trees. The herd might have
stopped in the grove to feed, for the trees are very
thick and evergreen. At the very least we will pick
up the trail there."

They began to walk, staying close beside the cliff,
picking their way over the mass of icy rubble. It
was difficult, but all of them felt safer without deep
snow around them.

At first Rowan leaned on Zeel's arm, as she had
suggested, but quite soon he was able to walk
alone, though he still felt weak. He was haunted by

the fear that the shadows would return, but Zeel remained close beside him, speaking to him often as if she knew he needed distraction from his thoughts.

It was broad daylight by the time they reached the end of the rubble, at a place where the cliff face curved to the right. As they rounded the corner and stumbled gratefully down to the smoother ground, they found themselves standing amid a jumble of bukshah tracks.

"There! You see?" Zeel exclaimed, pointing. And sure enough, the tracks headed directly for a bright patch of green—a grove of trees nestled hard against the cliff face.

They all began moving toward the grove as fast as they were able. The living green, startling against the dead gray, black, and white of the rest of the landscape, seemed to beckon them. But Rowan slowly realized that even if they had wished to turn aside from the grove they could not have done so. The ground on their left had begun to fall away steeply. Soon the black wall of the cliff face rose on one side of them, and a chasm yawned on the other. Like the bukshah before them, they had no choice but to go forward.

And the trees stretched across the path, filling it edge to edge.

Rowan's stomach began to flutter. The situation reminded him unpleasantly of the rock corridor before the vale of horrors. He could see that Zeel, Norris, and Shaaran were also becoming uneasy. Their brisk pace was slowing little by little, and their feet had begun to drag.

At last, as the trees loomed directly ahead, the four stopped. All instinctively raised their hands to their noses, for a strange, unpleasant smell, like the odor of bad eggs, hung in the air.

"I feel I have been herded to this place," Zeel said in a low voice. "I do not like it."

"Nor I," Norris agreed, peering into the trees. "Yet there seems no danger. The bukshah clearly entered without hesitation. You can see that by their tracks."

"The bukshah went through the vale of horrors, too," Shaaran reminded him. "Just because a place is safe for beasts, it does not mean it is safe for us."

"It may not even be safe for beasts," Zeel said, glancing at Rowan. "The bukshah entered the grove, but we do not know if they ever left it. That smell—"

"It is not the smell of death," Rowan broke in quickly. But a feeling of dread was growing within him. He was certain that the bukshah were very near. He sensed them. But the grove was utterly silent.

"Star!" he called.

The shout echoed dismally around the cliffs and died away without response.

"They may have left the grove long ago and be out of hearing," Shaaran whispered, plucking at his sleeve.

Rowan realized that she was trying to comfort him, but he could not answer her. He was tingling with the urge to plunge forward into the trees at once. But he knew his companions would follow. He could not drag them after him in a heedless rush into danger. He had to be cautious, find out all he could before going ahead, though it was agony to him to wait.

It was impossible to see very far into the grove. Many dead trees had fallen from the cliff top above, tangling with the branches of the living trees in the grove to form a low, thick canopy that shut out light from above.

The first few rows of trees were visible, however, and Rowan looked at them carefully. Certainly they did not look dangerous, and nothing like the killer trees of Unrin.

They were all of one type—sturdy though not

very tall, with spreading branches and glossy, well-shaped leaves. The only difference between them was in their bark. The trees that grew at the outer edges of the grove had rough, shaggy gray bark. But the gray bark only appeared in patches on the trees farther toward the center, and the trunks and branches of the trees right in the middle, on either side of the bukshah trail, were quite smooth and white.

Perhaps the outer trees need more protection than the inner ones do, Rowan thought. Perhaps the grove makes its own heat. For he had noticed that the air was warmer here, and there was little snow on the trees or on the ground around them.

And this was strange.

"We have been climbing steadily all morning," Zeel said, putting his thoughts into words. "We are higher on the Mountain now. It should be colder here, not warmer."

There was a short, anxious silence.

"What should we do?" exclaimed Norris.

And instantly Rowan felt the medallion grow hot as fire.

16 ⚬ The Grove

This time the rhyme came more easily. The burning, choking feeling was much less, and the voice sounded like Rowan's own. But somehow this made the experience even more horrible. Rowan's stomach heaved as helplessly he mouthed words that were as new and strange to him as they were to his companions:

"Make haste, your way is straight ahead.
Cast aside the fallen dead.
Life will ebb if you despair.
Sickness heals, and foul makes fair."

As the last word fell from his lips he braced himself, determined not to sink to the ground. But he need not have worried. Zeel, Norris, and Shaaran had gathered around him, ready to support him.

"Sheba said, 'Learn what it is to be what I am,' " he murmured, looking around at them. "I know now, only too well. And I wish I did not."

"Anyone of sense would feel the same," Norris said bluntly. "I beg your pardon, Rowan. I should have watched my tongue. And it was all for nothing. That accursed riddle offered us little help and less hope."

Cast aside the fallen dead.

Rowan shivered.

"The rhyme told us to move straight ahead and to make haste, Norris," Zeel snapped. "It also told us not to despair. These things at least we can understand. For the rest, we will see."

She turned to Rowan. "Are you able to move on?"

For answer he stepped forward, into the shadow of the trees. The others crowded after him.

They began to follow the bukshah tracks, the smooth white trunks of the trees rising on either side of them like guideposts. White boughs laced over their heads. They kept close together, their eyes and ears strained for any sudden sound or movement. But all was still, and as the trees closed in around them the silence and the shade grew deeper.

They said little to one another, and when they

did speak, it was in whispers. Soon the tangled canopy had become so low that Norris had to limp along with his shoulders bowed and his head bent. A light mist hung in the dimness, mingling with the mist of their breath, and the evil smell they had noticed earlier was becoming stronger.

Then Rowan saw a glimmer of light ahead. His heart thudded. Had they reached the end of the grove already?

"Zeel!" he whispered.

"I see it," she hissed from behind him. "It is some sort of clearing, I think. And the smell is coming from there, I am sure of it."

Rowan had to force himself not to break into a run. His breath was coming fast. The skin of his chest and back had begun prickling and itching unbearably. I am sweating, he thought. The cloak is too warm for this place. But he did not even consider pausing to take it off.

Soon the clearing was very near, but still Rowan could see little detail because of the thick mist that hung within it. He could only see shapes and colors. The ground was not flat but heaped with angular shapes of green and white. Amid the green and white there were patches of gray and one of black. There was no movement anywhere.

Rowan began moving faster.

"Take care," Zeel warned from behind him. "Rowan—"

Then Shaaran screamed.

Rowan and Zeel both swung around. Shaaran was clawing frantically at her shoulder, her face alive with horror. Norris was trying vainly to help her. "Get it off!" Shaaran was shrieking. "Help me!"

"What is it?" Zeel said sharply. "Shaaran, be still. Take your hands away. We cannot see—"

"They are on you, too!" Shaaran cried, shuddering with revulsion. "Oh, they are everywhere! Oh, horrible!"

Then Rowan's skin crawled as he saw, beneath her clutching fingers, a gray, rough-skinned, star-shaped thing fastened to her shoulder. Flattened against the ragged wool of her cloak, it was perfectly disguised, almost invisible. But now he had seen it he could see others—one on her side, and yet another on her arm.

On Zeel's arm, too. And on the back of her neck. And there, clinging to Norris's hood, were two more!

Where had they come from?

As the question raced through his mind, the tree branch above Shaaran's head seemed to move, and a flabby, star-shaped piece of bark peeled away and dropped quietly onto her back.

"The—the bark on the trees," Rowan stuttered. "It is not bark. It is—they are—"

His chest prickled. Filled with sudden, terrible suspicion he looked down and shouted aloud in horrified disgust. His chest was covered in a mass of shaggy gray. Some of the creatures were still wriggling, still settling into place. Others were firmly attached, and had clearly been so for some time, for they were swollen and plump.

Plump with his blood!

Frantically Rowan tried to pull the things away. Needle-sharp pains shot through his flesh as he tugged, but the gray things clung.

"Heat your knife in the torch flame, Rowan!" he heard Zeel shouting. "Hot metal will surely make them break their grip."

As Rowan fumbled for his knife, an overhanging branch brushed his wrist and another of the creatures slid onto the back of his hand.

With a cry he flung out his arm. The creature flew spinning away. But as he looked after it, he saw that the canopy was swarming with others. And hundreds more were still leaving the trunks of the trees beyond the pathway, climbing upward to join the crowd moving stealthily toward him and his companions.

"Run!" he gasped. "Out of the trees!"

They ran, stumbling clumsily toward the clearing, their heads down, their cloaks wrapped about them, shuddering and sobbing with horror.

And as they threw themselves out of the crawling green shade, onto a foul-smelling, steaming heap of dead trees tangled with vines, they saw the bukshah.

The beasts were lying near the center of the litter, as still as stones. Their shaggy bodies were covered with star-shaped creatures so swollen, and fitted so closely together, that it was hard to tell where one ended and the other began.

Star lay at the head of the herd. Her mighty horns were smeared with mud and wedged under a log. She was covered with feasting parasites.

With a cry of anguish Rowan dropped his torch and leaped forward, clambering over the fallen wood, careless of the thorny vines that tangled and tore at him. He reached Star and fell to his knees beside her, calling her name.

Her small black eyes opened. She rumbled softly, deep in her throat. A sound of love and trust.

Rowan's heart gave a great thud of disbelieving joy.

"She is alive!" he shouted, his voice cracking. "Star is still alive! The others! Perhaps they, too . . . they, too. . . ."

He swung around to the bukshah behind him. It

was Treasure, the only black bukshah in the herd, born in Rin's last spring. Treasure's eyes were closed, and he made no sound as Rowan touched his nose. But he was warm. Still warm, and breathing!

If Treasure, so young and small, still lived, there was hope for all the others. Frantically Rowan crawled between the still, gray bodies. He called the beasts by name, caressing them wherever he could put a hand. And at the sound of his voice and the touch of his fingers, warm skin twitched, eyelids fluttered, and the beasts groaned and sighed.

But it was almost too late. He knew it. He had seen it in Star's dull eyes, heard it in her feeble voice.

How long had it been since the bukshah walked through the grove, taking their time, stopping to eat the green leaves along their way? How long had it been since the star-shaped creatures clinging to the trees on either side of the track had slipped onto their backs, leaving the tree trunks in the center of the grove smooth and white?

Rowan could guess how it had been. By the time the bukshah stumbled out of the trees, they were all covered with parasites and weakening fast. Star had tried to lead them across the clearing, but one by one they had fallen. And they had lain here helpless ever since, slowly being drained of life.

He started up, looking wildly around him. He was

dizzy, and for a moment his eyes would not focus. Where were Zeel, Shaaran, and Norris? Why had they not come to help him?

He could not believe it when he saw they were still where he had left them. Shaaran was on her knees, her face white as chalk. Norris was bending over her, looking sick and panic-stricken. Zeel stood beside them.

"Help me, Zeel!" Rowan roared. "Bring the torch! Make haste!"

Zeel shook her head and beckoned. Inwardly raging at the delay, Rowan began clambering back toward them over the sea of fallen trees.

They came to meet him, moving slowly.

"You must help me!" he burst out as at last they came together. "The bukshah are dying! I need—"

"It is no use, Rowan," Zeel broke in quietly. "Do you think we have been standing idle? We have been trying to remove the vile things from our own bodies. And we cannot. It is as though they are made of stone. My dagger does not harm them, cold, warm, or red hot."

He gaped at her. "But—but surely . . . "

She shook her head. "Even naked flame does no good. I have tried it." Ruefully she showed him her arm. Two hideous star-shaped creatures clung there, unmarked, in the center of a great patch of charred cloth and raw, blistered skin.

"Zeel!" Rowan breathed.

Shaaran gave a choking sob, and Norris grimaced. "She did it before we could stop her," he said grimly.

Zeel shrugged. "I had to try it," she said. "These things are sucking the life out of us."

"And it will not take long for them to finish the job, I fear," said Norris. "If they can fell the bukshah in a day, how much more easily will they finish us?"

Shaaran had slumped onto a log, her face shadowed with despair.

Life will ebb if you despair.

"Wait!" Rowan exclaimed. "We have forgotten the rhyme!"

Shaaran looked up, her eyes startled. Slowly she repeated the words:

"Make haste, your way is straight ahead.
Cast aside the fallen dead.
Life will ebb if you despair.
Sickness heals, and foul makes fair."

"Truly, our lives, and the lives of the bukshah, will ebb away if we give up," Norris said. "That line at least I can understand. What of the rest? Do the first lines mean that we must leave the beasts to their fate and go forward if we are to save ourselves?"

Rowan gnawed at his lip. That idea had occurred to him, but he did not want to believe it.

"If we go straight ahead, that only means that we cross the clearing and go on through the trees on the other side," Zeel said. "But the trees over there are thick with the star creatures. Every trunk is gray."

"Perhaps the creatures cannot live outside the grove," Shaaran suggested suddenly. "Perhaps, if we can leave it, we will be free of them."

Norris looked hopeful, but Zeel shook her head. "I think you will find they can live wherever there are trees to support them," she said. She pointed at the dead tree Shaaran was sitting on and at the other trees lying about them. The white trunks were studded with faded star-shaped marks.

"These trees have died and fallen from the cliff top," Zeel went on. "And clearly the star creatures once lived on them, just as they live on the trees here. They suck sap, perhaps," she added calmly, "until richer food comes their way."

Rowan saw Shaaran grow even paler. "Perhaps it is because the trees on the cliff top died that the trees in the grove are so heavily infested," he said quickly. "If the trees above died and fell—"

And in a blinding flash, he saw the answer.

"The fallen dead!" he said. "The *trees*! The dead trees lying here, in this clearing. *They* are what we must cast aside!"

"But why?" Zeel asked blankly.

"Because there is something *beneath* them!" Norris exclaimed. "Something that will help us! And—"

"But the clearing is *heaped* with dead trees!" Zeel objected. "We cannot possibly move them all. Not in time. Not—"

"We do not have to move them all," said Rowan. His heart swelling, he turned and looked toward the place where Star lay. He knew without a doubt that Star would have fought her weakness to the end. She would have tried to save the herd. And she had collapsed with her muddy horns still locked beneath a tree trunk.

"There!" He pointed. "There, where Star lies, and the mist and the smell are strongest. That is where we must clear the fallen dead. Whatever lies below them is the answer!"

17 ✑ Foul Makes Fair

Rowan was desperate, Zeel was determined, and Shaaran did not spare herself. But all of them were growing weaker by the moment, and the task would have been hopeless if it had not been for Norris.

Norris saw at once that they could not move the fallen trees by brute force. Instead he tied ropes to them, then found long, straight branches they could use as levers to prise the white trunks up while the ropes were pulled.

Zeel and Shaaran took charge of the ropes, Norris and Rowan the levers. Sweating and straining, the companions pushed and pulled to Norris's command till, with a creaking, cracking sound, each tree shifted little by little from the place where it had lain for so long.

For hours they labored, as the light slowly dimmed in the sky above them. They moved one tree after another aside, uncovering nothing but more broken, tangled branches, more sad, uprooted trunks.

Norris's face was gray, set in deep lines of pain. The wound in his side had reopened, his injured leg could hardly support him. But he would not rest, would not stop. Again he placed the levers, tied the ropes. Again he gave his orders and began limping to his place, ready to heave once more.

One to fight, Rowan thought distantly. But Norris will never recover from this. Perhaps none of us will. Perhaps this is how our story ends.

He could feel his mind clouding. He knew that the creatures that clung to him were draining his strength and his will. He watched unsurprised as, without warning, Norris stumbled, swayed, and then crumpled slowly to the ground between Star and Treasure. Shaaran's cries rang in his ears like distant bells as she ran to her brother and bent over him.

Rowan met Zeel's eyes.

"Once more," she said, and wound her rope around her hand.

He nodded dully, and moved to the place where Norris would have stood. He took hold of the long branch jammed beneath the tree trunk.

"Now!" he called. And summoning the last of his

strength, the last of his hope and will, he pushed down.

For a long moment, nothing happened. Then the tree moved. Rowan heard Zeel's grunt of triumph, saw the rope straining. He pushed again, pushed with all his strength. But there was resistance. Something was holding the tree down. Something . . .

"Shaaran!" he shouted. "Help us! Here!"

He did not really believe Shaaran would come. But she did. Tear-stained, pale as a ghost, she slipped in front of him and threw her tiny weight onto the branch.

And it was enough. There was a sucking, groaning sound. The tree rolled aside. And as it did, a great, solid mat of rotten wood, vines, and dead leaves moved with it, and foul-smelling steam billowed from the place where it had lain.

Dizzy, staggering with weariness, Rowan, Zeel, and Shaaran stared at the thing they had uncovered.

It was a pool of bubbling, steaming water. Star and Norris lay in the mud at its edge.

Shaaran sat down suddenly, her eyes wide with shock.

Cautiously Zeel leaned forward and tested the water with the tip of a finger.

"It is hot!" she said in awe. "Water bubbling hot

from the ground! It is a miracle!" She sat back on her heels, wrinkling her nose. "But oh, it is foul. It stinks like a thousand eggs gone stale."

Sickness heals, and foul makes fair.

Rowan was speechless, consumed with desperate hope. He knelt beside Star and cautiously dipped his cupped hands into the spring. He felt warmth and a mild tingling, but nothing more. He lifted his hands, brimming with cloudy water, and held them close to Star's nose.

"Star," he whispered. "Is this what you were seeking? Is this what will help you? Help us?"

Star's eyes opened. She saw the water dribbling through Rowan's fingers. She snuffled as its odor reached her nostrils. She began struggling to rise.

But she did not lick Rowan's hands, only rubbed her nose against them, so Rowan knew that the water was not to be drunk, but bathed in.

"Zeel!" he cried. "Your arm! Put it into the water!"

Zeel plunged her injured arm deep into the spring. She held it there for the count of three. And when she drew it out, the star creature had fallen away and was bobbing, curled and dead, amid the bubbles on the spring's surface.

This Rowan had been hoping for. But what he had not been expecting, what made him gasp with wonder, and Shaaran cry aloud, was that Zeel's burned, blistered skin was whole and smooth again.

Zeel herself was looking down at her arm in amazement. "I—cannot believe it!" she stammered. "I cannot—"

"It is like magic!" whispered Shaaran. "It is like the magic spring in the fairyland Grandfather used to tell me of, long ago." Hope sprang into her face, flaring there like a candle flame. She scrambled over the mud to her brother.

Zeel and Rowan sprang to help her, and together they wrestled Norris's limp, heavy body into the spring.

Norris woke at the touch of the water. He flailed in panic, groaning and coughing. Then suddenly he grew still. His face changed. His eyes opened, free of pain, round with surprise.

Leaving him to Zeel and Shaaran, Rowan swung back to Star. She was still struggling to rise, with a bravery that nearly broke his heart. Tears sprang into his eyes as vainly he tried to help her.

Then Norris, Shaaran, and Zeel were with him, all of them dripping wet, all of them free of parasites, their eyes clear and shining. As they, too, bent over Star, the water streaming from their hair and clothes ran over her body. And wherever the water fell, star-creatures curled and dropped away.

Star groaned with relief, struggled again, and at

last found her feet. She stood, thin and swaying, by the bubbling pool. But she did not at once move into the water. Instead she bellowed, calling the herd, commanding them to hear her.

The other bukshah stirred. Everywhere ears flickered feebly, dull eyes opened. Star bellowed again. Then suddenly she lunged forward, collapsing into the center of the pool with a mighty splash, sinking beneath the surface.

Water rose in a great wave, surging over the muddy bank, drenching Treasure and a dozen other beasts and spraying the clearing like warm, muddy rain. The surface of the spring seemed to boil as Star sank deeper, deeper . . . .

With a cry of fear Rowan plunged after her. The smell of the water burned in his nose, caught in his throat, making him choke and gag. Frantically he strained to see beneath the bubbling, leaf-fouled surface. He caught a glimpse of something pale far below him and dived, eyes screwed tightly shut, hands outstretched, feeling his way blindly.

He felt a sudden, stinging pain as the point of one of Star's horns pierced his palm. He slid his hand down, took a firmer grip, and held on. He pulled with all his strength, but Star was like a huge stone. He could not lift her. His lungs were bursting.

He felt something dragging at his cloak. Someone

was trying to pull him upward, but he was anchored by his own grip on Star, and he would not let go.

Then suddenly there was movement from below him, and in a rush of bubbles he was propelled up, up into the light. His head broke through the surface, and he gasped for air. His ears were ringing. As he opened his blurred eyes, the first thing he saw was Norris's sleek, drenched head bobbing beside him. Norris still had hold of his cloak. Norris was trying to drag him toward the bank, mouthing words he could not hear.

Then both of them were tumbled sideways as in a shower of spray Star's massive body surfaced almost directly below them. With a stab of joy Rowan saw the great bukshah lift her head clear of the water and begin swimming powerfully. Her eyes were bright, her horns were gleaming white, water streamed from her woolly mane. Rowan shouted, choked, and shouted again, but to his amazement, as he tried to reach out for her, Star nudged him vigorously aside, into the shallows.

He found his feet, then fell to his knees, dizzy with hurt and confusion. He felt Norris heave at him. He heard Star bellow. And finally his ringing ears made sense of Norris's shouts.

"Get out, Rowan!" Norris was bawling. "You will be crushed! Make way for them!"

Then Rowan saw that Star was not the only buk-shah in the spring. Treasure was already up to his neck in water. Two other calves—Misty and Sprite—were splashing unsteadily after him. Three more were following. And behind them were the other members of the herd, thin, weak, and stag-gering, star creatures covering them like hideous armor except where they had been sprayed by Star's first mighty plunge into the water.

Frantically the huge, ragged beasts pushed for-ward, deaf and blind to everything except the spring. Norris hauled Rowan out of their path, and an instant later hoofs were trampling the mud where the two had lain.

In threes and fours the bukshah sank into the deep water, moaning with relief as the parasites left them, then raising their heads and swimming to the opposite side of the spring, where Star now stood waiting for them.

And when all of them had made the crossing, when all were standing, steaming and dripping, on the other side of the spring, Rowan, Zeel, Shaaran, and Norris collected their possessions, and followed them.

They stayed that night in the clearing, the buk-shah all around them. Despite being soaked through, they were not cold, for the air beside the spring was as warm as a summer afternoon in Rin, though it did not smell as sweet.

They lit a fire, heated a little water for tea, and toasted bread to eat with cheese and honey. And as the sun set, they lay down and slept well and deeply, for they knew that here at least the ice creepers could not come.

It was still dark when Rowan woke. Star's nose was nudging his cheek. Her great curved horns, sharpened to knife points on the rock walls before the vale of horrors, loomed too close to his eyes for comfort.

"Star, why do you wake me so soon?" he mumbled, rolling over. "Dawn must be hours away."

Star rumbled to him and pawed the ground, then turned away. He sat up and saw that the other beasts were already standing, waiting. He watched as Star passed through them and began to lead the way into the trees.

The herd was on the move again. Quickly Rowan roused Norris, Shaaran, and Zeel. Each of the companions took a hurried sip of water and a handful of dried berries. Then they lit torches, shouldered their packs, and followed the bukshah, even Zeel still rubbing the sleep from her eyes.

The path through the trees beyond the spring was cluttered with dead wood, but the bukshah pushed through every obstacle, crushing it underfoot, clearing the way. The four strolled after them, reveling in the luxury of renewed strength and freedom from pain.

The torchlight flickered on the trees, flickered on star creatures thickly clustered on trunks and branches, but few of the parasites tried to settle on the humans or the beasts. Those that did paid instantly for their mistake, falling dead as they touched hair and garments still damp with the water of the spring.

Slowly the dampness disappeared in the forest warmth, and Rowan began to fear. But still the star creatures held back, and still the people and the beasts walked in peace, as if the water had given them a protective coating.

It was like a walk in a dream, and it ended only too quickly. The sun was still far below the horizon when Rowan, Zeel, Shaaran, and Norris stepped out of the trees, but they could see well enough the bleak and brutal place of icy rock to which they had come.

They were standing on the only level place in a landscape of sharp angles. Boulders cluttered the sloping ground ahead. To their right rose the cliffs, wreathed in mist, capped with dead trees and snow. The sheer, black cliff walls were half hidden by the tumble of huge, jagged rocks and dead trees piled against them.

To the left all was darkness, but Rowan could see

that the ground sloping away from the area where they stood was steep and barren. And, somehow, dreadfully familiar.

Zeel shivered. "We have reached the Mountain's western face," she said in a low voice. "Below is the Pit of Unrin."

18 ∞ Before Dawn

Shaaran cowered a little closer to Norris. "What—what is the Pit of Unrin?" she stammered. She had heard many tales since arriving in Rin, but not this one. No one spoke willingly of the Pit of Unrin.

Rowan moistened his lips. "It is a place of doom . . . a dead valley filled with flesh-eating trees," he said. "Once it was the Valley of Gold. A great people lived there, ancient allies of the Travelers and the Maris."

"The Valley of Gold!" exclaimed Norris. "But that was the place Timon and Neel the potter spoke of at the meeting! The place of the people who turned their backs on the Mountain and caused the first Cold Time."

The air seemed to darken. A small, cruel wind

blew about them, nipping at their faces, tugging at the torch flames, tweaking the shaggy hair of the bukshah who were wandering among the rocks like lost souls, pawing the ground.

We have arrived, Rowan thought suddenly. This is the journey's end.

"The Cold Time happened in the land's earliest days," Zeel said slowly. "The people of the Valley of Gold lived on in peace and plenty long, long after it ended. Then, suddenly, they were no more. For centuries it was not known what had happened to them. Now we know that the killer trees overtook the Valley and killed them all. Ogden thinks that the tree roots then undermined this part of the Mountain, causing the cliffs above to crumble and partly fall."

"How could a whole people, rich and happy, just disappear?" murmured Shaaran, staring down at the blackness below. "Did they not call for aid? Did the Travelers not—"

"The Travelers were far away," Zeel said, her face somber. "They had made camp on the coast near Maris for the cold season, as always. The first winds of winter brought a Zebak invasion. The Travelers fought alongside the Maris people to defend the land, but the Zebak were many and the Maris were weak and divided, for their leader, the Keeper of the Crystal, was dying. Urgent word was sent to the Valley of Gold. The Valley people had never failed to answer a call to arms."

"But this time they did not come?" Norris was leaning forward, fascinated as he always was by tales of battle.

Zeel shook her head. "They did not come, and the Traveler messengers never returned. It is thought the messengers died of cold before reaching their goal. The snow was early and plentiful that year."

She turned away to look at the bukshah. Rowan did not prompt her. Zeel had no relish for tales of war. Though she pretended otherwise, the seemingly endless battle between her natural and her adopted peoples caused her much grief.

Norris had no such fine feelings. "So what happened then?" he demanded. "Go on, Zeel! The beasts are resting, it seems, or cannot decide which way to go. What else have we to do but talk?"

Zeel looked back at him and smiled wryly as she saw that he would give her no peace until the story had been completed.

"The city of Maris quickly fell to the enemy, and the Maris people were forced to flee into tunnels beneath the sea where their leader could still protect them," she said quietly. "The Zebak tried to take the Travelers as slaves, but the tribe slipped out of their clutches like shadows and escaped, going into hiding in the north."

She grimaced. "We can only guess what happened then, for neither Maris nor Travelers were there to see it. But when the Travelers returned to Maris in spring, they found that many of the Zebak ships had already been sent home—loaded with looted Maris goods, no doubt, for the city was stripped bare. The Zebak who remained thought that the war had been won."

She shook her head at their folly. "For the Travelers, of course, the struggle had only just begun. They sent fresh messengers to the Valley of Gold and began to harry the enemy in any way they could. Ambushes and raids. Thefts of food and arms. Disturbances night after night . . ."

She had all her companions' full attention now. Shaaran was listening to the story as intently as Rowan and Norris were.

"Starved of food and sleep, menaced by an enemy they could not see, the Zebak were soon jumping at shadows," Zeel went on. "Then what the Travelers had been waiting for took place. The old, weak Keeper died. A new Keeper took his place, and the magic Crystal of Maris flamed anew. The Maris people came up from the tunnels, united and filled with new hope. By this time the Zebak were no match for them. And so at last the enemy was defeated and driven away."

She frowned, looking down over the bleak slopes that disappeared into blackness. "But in the midst of the rejoicing, the new messengers returned from the center, and triumph turned to sorrow as they told what they had found. Above the Valley of Gold, the face of the Mountain had changed to a mass of rubble, as if two giants had battled there. The Valley had gone. In its place was the horror later named the Pit of Unrin—a shadowed mass of hideous trees that seemed to breathe evil. And the people of the Valley had vanished from the earth."

Rowan gave a great sigh. He had heard the old story many times before, but never like this. Somehow Zeel's flat, matter-of-fact voice had made the details of the tale stand out as Ogden's colorful and dramatic recounting never had.

Shaaran put his thoughts into words. "Chance truly played a fearful part in that history," she said. "If the Zebak had attacked a few weeks earlier . . . if the snows had not come sooner than expected . . . if the messengers had reached the Valley of Gold . . . the Valley people would have gone to the coast to fight and would not have been killed by the trees of Unrin."

"They might have been killed by the Zebak instead," Norris said grimly. "Who knows? There is no point in ifs, Shaaran. But here is another one for you: If the people of the Valley of Gold had not died out, they could have told us what is in store for us. They could have told us how *they* made peace with the Mountain and ended the first Cold Time."

Zeel sighed, her eyes drifting once again to the bukshah. "That knowledge is lost in the mists of time," she said. "The Valley people did not share it with their friends. Perhaps they were too proud. Or ashamed. Ogden knows many old secrets, but when I asked him of this one, he could not tell me anything."

Could not tell you, or *would* not? Rowan asked himself silently. A picture of Ogden's dark, hawk-like face floated into his mind—Ogden's face as it had been at their very first meeting, Ogden's black eyes intently searching his own.

Ogden the Storyteller, leader of the Travelers, had been interested in Rowan from the beginning. Far more interested than might have been expected by Rowan or anyone else.

Why? Why had Ogden probed his mind so deeply on that first meeting, wanting to know every trivial thing about Rowan's parents, the bukshah, and the life he led?

In his heart Rowan knew the answer. He had known it ever since the night in the cave. Now he faced it squarely.

Ogden had sensed something. Sensed that, however unlikely it seemed, the puny, quaking boy before him was fated to play an important part in the story of the land they shared.

The storyteller had proved a firm ally. But always it had been as if he was holding something back— some secret knowledge or suspicion he could not bring himself to voice.

He had not been surprised when Rowan brought Shaaran and Norris from the land of the Zebak. He seemed to have been expecting it. Only when the silks were unrolled, and the people of Rin began exclaiming and wondering over them, had he seemed troubled, pressing his thin lips together and turning away.

Perhaps in that moment Ogden realized that what he had been waiting for, what he had feared, had already begun. That Rowan had unknowingly set in train a series of events that would end . . .

End here, Rowan thought, looking around at his companions, gazing past them at the shadowy forms of the bukshah milling aimlessly among the rocks. End here, for good or ill.

"Dawn is not long away," Zeel said suddenly.

Rowan swung around to look at her. There had been something in her voice . . .

"What is it?" he whispered.

Zeel was standing stiffly, her head up. The torch she held threw yellow light on her high cheekbones, her strong, straight brows. "I do not know," she said, her lips barely moving.

What is happening? Rowan thought desperately. What must I do?

And he felt the medallion grow warm at his throat. His skin began to prickle and the hideous, familiar sickness flooded through him.

No, he thought with dread. No!

But he knew it was no use. He had asked his question. The thing would happen whether he willed it or not.

He felt the torch drop from his numb fingers, heard Zeel's muffled exclamation as she turned to him. His mouth opened. His lips began to move, shaping the words.

"When earthbound thunder greets the day,
The breaking heart will clear the way.
And where the golden river flows,
The hidden stair its secret shows."

As he spoke the last line, memory flooded

through him—memory of a dream, a terrifying dream that he had forgotten until this moment. He had been climbing a stone stairway toward a gaping mouth at the top, following the bukshah.

His head was spinning. He could not think.

When had he dreamed this? How could he have forgotten it? Was the memory true or false?

Wait, he told himself. Wait . . .

Slowly the dizziness and sickness ebbed. His mind cleared. He became aware that he was sagging against Zeel, that her arm was around him and that Norris was supporting him from the other side. Gently he pushed them away to stand on his own feet.

He had remembered. The dream of the stone stairway had come to him in the cave. The fear of being trapped, the escape from the cave, and everything that had happened since had driven it from his mind. But now the memory had come back, dark and fearful.

All the other dreams had come true, in every way that mattered. So this nightmare would come true also. And soon.

When earthbound thunder greets the day . . .

When the Dragon of the Mountain roared at dawn?

Rowan's ears were buzzing. Dazedly he stared up

at the misty cliff tops. Slowly his eyes moved downward.

And stopped.

Was it his imagination, or could he see a faint blur of lighter color on the cliff face? He squinted and became more and more sure that he was right. There was something—some mark or fault—just above the place where the steep slope of rocks began.

If he had not had the dream, he would have thought that the rocks were the stair of the rhyme. But he *had* had the dream, and he knew they were not. The bukshah could not climb those rocks.

The stair—the hidden stair—was here somewhere, masked by shadows.

The bukshah knew it. That was why they would not move from this place. That was why they were milling among the rocks at the base of the pile, pawing the ground. The stairway was here, and they could not find it.

But at dawn the secret would be revealed. The rising sun would illuminate the rocks. The stairway, now hidden, would be bathed in a golden river of light.

It will happen, Rowan thought. I need do nothing but wait. He felt strangely calm.

"Why does he not answer?" The buzzing in his

ears shaped itself suddenly into words, and he recognized Norris's voice, sharp with panic. He realized that his companions had been calling him for long minutes, trying to make him speak.

He turned toward the sound. Three anxious faces floated in the dimness. Zeel. Shaaran. Norris.

Slowly he realized that there *was* something he had to do. Before the dawn broke. Before the Dragon roared. Before the sun exposed the stairway and he began the last, long climb to meet his destiny.

It *will* happen, he told himself. But it need not happen to all of us. In the dream I saw no one on the stair but myself and the bukshah.

An immense loneliness descended upon him. His chest ached.

The breaking heart will clear the way.

He had wondered what that meant. Now he knew.

He opened his dry lips. "It is time for you to leave me," he said, his voice sounding strange and croaking to his own ears. "What must be done now, I must do alone."

19 ～ Decisions

Shaaran, Norris, and Zeel protested, as Rowan knew they would. The rhyme had shaken them, but it had not shaken their will or their loyalty.

He knew there was only one way to convince them. He had to tell them of his nightmare about the stone stairway and the steaming, gaping mouth at its top. He shrank from it, for if they were to believe that what he had dreamed would certainly come to pass, he would have to confess to the other dreams that had come true—the dreams he had kept secret all this time.

It will destroy their trust in me, he thought, the pain in his heart growing stronger. It will break our friendship. But . . . but perhaps that is all to the good. Their love and loyalty bind them to me. If those ties are cut, they will be free to leave. The return to Rin will be perilous, but they will have water from the grove to aid them. And nothing is more perilous than remaining here.

"You do not understand," he said loudly, breaking in on their protests. "And that is because—because I have deceived you."

The babble of voices ceased abruptly. He saw three startled pairs of eyes staring at him, and bowed his head.

He took a deep breath to steady himself, and in a low voice confessed everything. He spoke rapidly, forcing himself to stick to the bare bones of the story. No one interrupted.

"I should have told you from the first but did not, for my own selfish reasons," Rowan finished awkwardly, without raising his eyes. "I wanted our friendship to stay as it had always been. I did not want you to regard me with disgust or to fear me as people do Sheba. I have always felt a stranger among my people. Now I feel a freak. But that is no excuse. I am sorry."

There was silence. It lasted so long that Rowan half wondered whether the three had already moved silently away, leaving him alone. He forced himself to look up.

They were standing in front of him, exactly as

they had been before he began his speech. Their faces were grave. Shaaran had tears in her eyes. At that moment Rowan almost wished they *had* gone without a word.

Then Shaaran flung herself into his arms.

"I cannot believe you have borne this burden alone, all this time, for our sake, Rowan," she cried. "Never could I have done it!"

"Nor I," said Norris, shaking his head and clasping Rowan's hand.

"Perhaps I could," said Zeel calmly. "But I thank the heavens that I did not have to try."

Stunned, Rowan stared at them. Their reaction was so different from the one he had expected that he was tongue-tied.

"I knew you were keeping something to yourself, Rowan, but I could not think what could be so fearful that you would need to hide it," Zeel said. "That is something I still do not quite understand, for why would anyone turn away from a good friend because he has an unexpected, and very useful, talent?"

"More a curse than a talent," Rowan managed to say.

"Curse or talent, it does not matter," said Shaaran, drawing back so she could look at him but still keeping hold of his arm. "You cannot divide a true friend into parts and say, 'This part I like, but that part I will not accept'! You take the package as a whole."

"And speaking of that, if you think you can divide the whole we four have become, and send three-quarters of it home while you go on alone, you are very much mistaken," Norris growled.

Shaaran nodded agreement. "I am not saying I am not afraid," she said. "I am very afraid. But this does not mean I wish to turn back."

"But—but did you not hear what I said?" stammered Rowan. "The dream of the stairway . . . there was dread in it. And death. I felt it."

"And so?" Zeel asked coolly. "This is not your decision to take, Rowan of the Bukshah. Whether you saw us in your dream or not, Sheba's rhyme stated clearly that four souls must follow the beasts."

She looked from Norris to Shaaran, then back to Rowan. "And follow them we will," she added, "wherever the path may lead us. Not for love of you, but for love of this land and everything we hold dear."

And, humbled, Rowan fell silent.

Norris cleared his throat. "Very well," he said briskly. "Now, let us think what we can do to help ourselves. Dream or no dream, I do not relish the idea of waiting here for dawn like a helpless victim who has no command at all over his fate."

"The stairway in Rowan's dream led to a gaping mouth," Zeel said. "The mouth, surely, must be the entrance to another cave."

"Must it?" Shaaran asked timidly. "But hot breath was steaming—"

"Dreams often show ordinary things in a strange way," Norris broke in. "The bukshah were also dreamlike—different from the way they really are. Is that not so, Rowan?"

Rowan hesitated. Norris was right, of course, but . . .

Zeel was looking up, squinting through the dimness. "That patch of gray is the only sign of an entrance I can see in the cliff face. If we climb to it now, we may learn something that will aid us later."

Shaaran made a small sound of protest, but Norris agreed instantly. For him, a hard climb was far preferable to waiting helplessly in the darkness. Rowan remained silent. He could see that Zeel's plan was sensible, but still he felt uneasy.

Perhaps I am just unsettled because matters have been taken out of my hands, he thought. Perhaps I have grown too used to being a leader.

The thought made him smile, despite his fears.

"I—I cannot possibly climb those rocks," Shaaran said in a small voice.

Norris snorted with laughter. "Of course not, Shaaran," he said. "No one expects you to. Zeel and I will see what is to be seen, then come back and report to you and Rowan."

Rowan felt a pang. This was all wrong. He knew it. But he could not forbid Zeel and Norris to try what they felt they must.

And neither can I wait here while they do it, he thought. I must see whatever is up there with my own eyes.

"If you are determined to do this, I will go with you," he said aloud. "I think I can manage the climb."

"But what of Shaaran?" exclaimed Norris. "She cannot stay here alone!"

"Of course I can!" Shaaran said with spirit. "I do not need a guard. I will stay here and keep watch. If any danger threatens, or the bukshah begin to stray, I will call you."

And so it was decided. In moments Zeel, Norris, and Rowan were threading their way toward the rocks directly beneath their goal.

Star tossed her head and lumbered forward as Rowan began climbing. It seemed to him that she would have tried to stop him if she could. But by the time she reached the base of the rock pile, he was already too high for her to reach.

He looked down at her. She was pawing at the

rocks as though she wanted to come after him. But she could not. The rock pile was much too steep for her. She stretched up her neck and bellowed dismally as he climbed higher.

Star does not like this any more than I do, Rowan thought uneasily. His foot slipped. Frantically he scrabbled for a handhold, saving himself by a miracle.

"Pay attention, Rowan!" Zeel called from above him. "These rocks are treacherous, especially in the dark! You cannot climb with half your mind on something else."

Rowan knew she was right. He forced everything from his mind but the task at hand, and climbed on.

At last they reached the top of the rock pile. The air had suddenly become very much colder. Freezing mist swirled above them, and Rowan shivered as he looked at the patch of gray in the cliff face before him. It was not the place he had seen in his dream. He did not know if he was glad or sorry.

The gray area was far larger and lighter than it had appeared from below, and now they could all see that it was not a hole at all, but part of the cliff wall itself.

Part of the cliff, yet not part. It was quite unlike the dark rock that surrounded it.

"What is it?" Norris whispered. He pulled off his

glove, stretched forward, and touched the gray material. A look of surprise crossed his face, and he snatched his hand away.

"I have never felt anything like it!" he exclaimed. "It is rough to touch, but far softer than rock. And it is not cold! It is only a little cooler than my fingers!"

"Norris, how could you be so foolhardy?" scolded Zeel. "It is probably some sort of fungus that has grown over the rock. You have no idea what damage it may do to you!"

Aghast, Norris began wiping his fingers vigorously on his cloak.

Zeel took out her dagger and stuck the point in the gray material. "If it is a fungus, it is very thick," she said, puzzled. She pushed the knife harder, and the shining blade slid forward, sinking to the hilt. Zeel jerked it back, twisting it, and a chunk of the gray material broke loose and fell onto her sleeve. She shook it off hurriedly.

"How strange," she murmured, her eyes alive with curiosity. Again she pushed the knife into the hole that now gaped in the gray and began scraping energetically.

"Leave it, Zeel," Rowan said, without much hope that she would listen to him. He glanced down, over his shoulder, to where the bukshah milled anxiously and Shaaran waited.

He could pick out Star among the herd. He could see Shaaran's pale, upturned face. His stomach turned over as he realized that the sky was lightening. Soon it would be dawn.

"Zeel!" he said, turning back toward the cliff. "Zeel, we had better—"

But Zeel was not listening. She had lifted herself up so that she was level with the gray material. Her eye was pressed against the hole she had made. As Rowan watched, she pushed herself back. Her face was expressionless.

"You had better look at this," she said evenly.

Rowan moved forward, but Norris was before him, eagerly putting an eye to the hole. There was a moment's silence, then Norris, too, pushed himself back.

"What is it?" Rowan exclaimed.

Norris was very pale. His eyes were almost black. His mouth moved, as though he wanted to speak, but no sound came.

His heart thumping like a drum, Rowan flung himself forward and looked through the hole.

At first he could see nothing but a dull blue blur. The cold was so intense that it made his eye ache and water.

So much colder inside than out, he thought. Yet the gray barrier is not cold in itself.

It came to him slowly that the gray material was a seal. Like the bukshah-skin cloak he wore, it was a powerful barrier against both heat and cold. It stopped one flowing into the other.

The gray material was filling a gap in the rock. It was being used to keep deathly cold in and less freezing air out.

But why is it here? he thought confusedly. Who made it?

Then his eyes adjusted to the strange blue light beyond the gray barrier, and he saw—

Saw a huge cavern, so large that the whole village of Rin could have fitted inside it four times over. Saw that the cavern's roof and walls were gleaming with the same white-blue fungus that he remembered from his journey within the Mountain years ago. Saw that the roof was studded with pale blobs that he slowly realized were the blunt, chewed ends of tree roots. Saw the entrances to other chambers, hundreds of other chambers, and tunnels leading upward, threading through the center of the Mountain.

And saw, with a thrill of horror, ice creepers.

Ice creepers in their tens of thousands. Ice creepers squirming through all of this vast space, coiling one on top of the other in a huge, moving mass of white. Ice creepers building, building relentlessly, sliding through the tunnels with working jaws, using the chewed material from their mouths to construct more and yet more of the gray cells that already lined the cavern's icy walls and rose in great towers to its roof.

The hollow core of the Mountain was a nest. A gigantic nest. In every finished cell lay a white worm—a tiny replica of the adults that tended it.

And then, in terror, Rowan saw the creatures nearest to him grow still, turn their blind heads toward him, open their jaws, and hurl themselves, hissing, against the spy hole.

20 ~ Earthbound Thunder

Rowan jerked back with such force that he almost lost his grip and fell. His companions' cries of shock, Shaaran's thin, echoing screams from below, rang in his ears as he clung by his fingertips to the sharp rock.

"Back!" he shouted. "They sensed me! They felt the warmer air. They are—"

In horror he saw tiny cracks running like spiderwebs out from the spy hole. He saw the gray material begin to crumble as the hole grew larger, larger—

Then he was scrambling downward, with Zeel and Norris, scrambling backward, the toes of his boots scrabbling for footholds, his hands aching, rock scraping rough and cold on his chest and legs.

But already the terrible head of an ice creeper was breaking through the gray barrier. Huge, ferocious, the creeper squirmed out onto the rocks and plunged after them. Freezing breath gushed from its mouth, filling the air before it with icy mist, coating the rocks with a film of white.

"Down!" Shaaran was screaming from below. "Get down!"

Down! Down! Down to where it was warmer. Where there were torches. Where the grove stood not far away.

Rowan slipped, recovered, slipped again. His breath was aching in his throat. Clutching desperately at the rock, he looked up.

The creeper was almost upon them, its blind head striking forward, its ghastly jaws gaping. It was so large that the tip of its tail still lashed the rocks at the top of the pile. And even in his terror Rowan marveled that the gray barrier in the cliff already gleamed whole and smooth again. The moment the ice creeper had fully emerged, the hole had been sealed behind it.

So quickly. The thought tumbled through Rowan's dazed mind as at last his foot found a cleft that would support it and his perilous clamber downward began again. His stomach churned as he thought of ice creepers rushing to the hole, their blunt heads stabbing at it while their gaping mouths spewed out the sticky gray material that would harden in moments, repairing the damage, sealing in the precious cold.

It would only take a few. A few among the tens of thousands of these hideous crawling things that infested the Mountain, tunneling through the rock, chewing the roots of the trees. Building, building . . .

Tens of thousands? Rowan heard himself groan aloud. *Hundreds* of thousands! And soon hundreds of thousands more. The creepers' tunnels honeycombed the Mountain's freezing rock. The cells of their wormlike young packed the Mountain's icebound caverns.

In the bitter chill of the Cold Time they would breed unceasingly, and their young would spread outward from the Mountain in their millions. Till every tree in the land had fallen dead, and every living thing had been destroyed.

He slid down a sheet of rock, landing with a thud on a blessedly flat boulder at its base. He took a shuddering breath. It was not so cold here, he was sure of it. He had moved out of the freezing air at the top of the rock pile into the warmer air below.

He dared to glance up and saw he was right. The ice creeper was slowing. It was swaying, hissing, clearly uncomfortable. But it was still coming. Rowan heard shouting, glanced around rapidly, and saw Norris and Zeel just a little below him. They were both looking down and calling. Norris was stretching out an arm to . . . to where a flame bobbed far below them. A flame moving upward!

Rowan realized that Shaaran was climbing toward them, a flaring torch clutched awkwardly in her hand. The girl's pale, terrified face seemed to float in the dimness behind the flame. Below her loomed the bukshah. The beasts were gathered in a tight, unmoving knot at the foot of the rock pile. Shaaran must have had to press her way through them to begin her climb.

And she is so afraid of them! Rowan thought. Then he almost laughed. Afraid of the bukshah, when the rocks were hard, high, and jagged, and an ice creeper hissed its rage above!

Yet he knew, none better, that small fears could be as terrifying as great ones. He knew that Shaaran had used all her strength in a desperate effort to take her companions what they needed to survive.

How easily she could slip and fall! In terror Rowan watched the wavering flame. He knew how difficult, how perilous, the climb up the rock slide was. And Shaaran, fragile and afraid, was doing it with one hand hampered by the torch she was carrying.

"Rowan!" Zeel's sharp cry made him jump. Instinctively he looked up again, to where the ice creeper writhed in a cloud of icy breath. His eyes caught movement above it, and his blood ran cold. The cliff face was almost hidden by billowing white mist. And in the mist hundreds of blue-white shapes were coiling, slithering heavily down from the snow-capped cliff top.

Of course, Rowan thought numbly. How could I have thought that only one creature would defend the nest? The gray door had to be sealed to keep the warmer air from entering the chamber. But higher up, where it is as cold outside as it is within, there would be no need for sealed doors. And through those openings more creepers are coming, coming in their hundreds.

He began scrambling downward again. Fear gripped him, but he gritted his teeth, fighting it back. He had to keep his mind on what he was doing, think only of placing his feet surely, of using his hands well. If he slipped and cracked a bone— even twisted his ankle—he was finished.

A hissing sound filled his ears. A draft of freezing mist engulfed him. He gasped and choked, looked up, and saw the first ice creeper rearing directly above him, its huge, snakelike body almost hidden in a white cloud.

Somehow it had gained the strength to brave the warmer air on the lower part of the rock pile.

And behind it were the others.

Rowan heard himself cry out in terror. The upper part of the rock pile was covered in billowing mist. The mist was crawling downward, and within it was a mass of hissing blue mouths, blue-white bodies writhing on rocks now gleaming with black ice.

They do not just thrive in the cold. They cause it! The more there are, the colder it grows. The thought pierced his mind like a dagger of ice. And a terrible knowledge followed swiftly.

Nowhere is safe from them.

The ice creeper lunged blindly. Rowan jerked back with a yell, letting go of his handhold, slipping, sliding, all caution gone. His heels struck rock, skidded forward and down. The next moment he was trapped waist high in a cleft between two boulders.

Terrified, struggling to haul himself free, he looked up. The creeper's mouth gaped wide above him. Its slanting teeth glistened as it struck down, reaching for him—

There was a ferocious shout, and Rowan, dazed with fear, saw a streak of fire blaze past his head and plunge straight into the yawning blue-lined jaws. The creeper reared back, the end of a torch still protruding from its mouth. Freezing dark blue mist gushed from its throat. Then it crumpled and fell.

Strong arms hauled Rowan out of the cleft, none too gently. "Make haste!" Norris roared in his ear.

The mass of white, coiling shapes on the rocks above them seemed to surge forward as Rowan and Norris half fell, half scrambled downward. When Rowan looked over his shoulder, he could see Shaaran and Zeel finishing their own panicky descent.

Do not fall, do not fall, he kept thinking, speaking as much to them as to himself. It was with relief that he saw the two girls sliding down the last steep rock to land safely in the midst of the bukshah herd. Instinctively he and Norris aimed for the same place.

But when at last they reached the bottom they found that the bukshah had moved, and Shaaran and Zeel had moved with them. They were now at the far end of the pile of rocks—the end farthest away from the grove. Zeel and Shaaran were standing strangely still, the bukshah pressed closely around them.

Shouting, Norris and Rowan ran to the place. The bukshah moved aside to let them pass, closing in silently behind them.

"Why are you here?" Norris panted when he reached Shaaran's side. She did not answer, just stared at him with huge, frightened eyes.

He tugged at her arm. "Do you not see? Creepers are coming in their hundreds! We must get back to the grove. It is our only chance!"

But as he turned, dragging Shaaran with him, he found his way blocked by the bukshah. The beasts had moved to enclose the newcomers in their circle, and now stood shoulder to shoulder around them like a solid, shaggy wall.

They snuffled and rumbled, nudging Rowan, Zeel, and Norris gently with their noses as though eager to touch them. But they did not touch Shaaran, keeping back from her as if they knew she was afraid.

Norris called and pushed at them in vain.

"Rowan!" he shouted, looking wildly around him. "Make them shift!"

Rowan knew there was no hope of that. Star was in the center of the group, right beside him. Her small black eyes were fixed upon him, and in those eyes he could see her determination. She would not let him pass.

The beasts are wiser than we know. . . .

Rowan felt the hair rise on the back of his neck.

"They will not move," Zeel said. "They pushed us here, and here they intend us to stay." Her voice was low. Her light eyes were fixed and intent. She seemed to be listening to something no one else could hear.

"What is it, Zeel?" Rowan whispered.

"Listen!" she replied.

Rowan listened. And he heard . . . nothing. Nothing but the beating of his own heart, Norris's heavy breathing, the slight scraping of the bukshah hoofs on the rocky ground.

The moaning wind had dropped. There was an eerie stillness, as though the Mountain were holding its breath. The silence seemed to press upon Rowan's ears and his eyes. His teeth began to ache. His skin prickled.

He forced himself to look up. The creepers on the rock pile had halted. Amid the swirling mist, their blunt heads waved uncertainly.

"What—?" Norris began, and choked, as his voice dried in his throat.

The light had changed. The sullen sky was stained with red. It was dawn.

High, high above them, in its ice cave on the peak, the Dragon roared.

And there came, from deep within the Mountain, a long, low growl like the rumbling of thunder.

The air shimmered before Rowan's eyes. The earth seemed to tremble beneath him.

Then the rocks began to fall. Slowly, like a child's castle made of wooden blocks, a castle tipped by a careless finger, the rocks toppled, crashing down upon one another, and upon the ice creepers thrashing helplessly in their path.

Faster the rocks tumbled as the Mountain quaked beneath them. Faster and faster they thundered down, crashing upon the place where only minutes ago the companions had stood, spinning over the edge of the drop into the Pit of Unrin, carrying the smashed and ruined bodies of the ice creepers with them.

Rowan fell to his knees, pressing his head against Star's shaggy side, hiding his eyes from the sight of the world coming apart around him, trying to shield his ears from the growling thunder.

But there was no escape from the sound. It was everywhere. Star's body was trembling with it. The earth was vibrating with it. It filled the air he breathed.

The sound! Rowan had never heard such a sound. Not from the Dragon of the Mountain. Not from the trees of Unrin. Not from the Great Serpent of Maris. The roar of the Mountain was loud and terrible, like a bellow of burning rage. And as Rowan cowered beneath it, it rose and rose until there was the shrieking, grating groan of splitting rock. Then a gale of hot breath swept over him, throwing him flat to the ground.

21 ∽ The Stairway

 Rowan's head was aching. His ears were ringing. Star's nose roughly nudged his cheek. Perhaps she had nudged it more gently many times before, trying to wake him. But now she could wait no longer. He could hear her rumbling anxiously, pawing the ground.

He opened his eyes. They watered and burned. Star loomed above him, a dark shape against the hazy sky. The terrible dawn had faded. It was daylight.

Slowly Rowan became aware of his surroundings.

Zeel, Norris, and Shaaran were stirring beside him. The other bukshah still surrounded them all, still formed that vast, living gray wall that had shielded them from the worst of the Mountain's fury. But the wall was ragged and swaying now, and the air was filled with rumbling and snorting.

The herd was impatient to be gone.

It is time, Rowan thought. He felt nothing. His mind was numb.

He clambered to his feet, trying to keep his swimming head steady, clinging to Star's mane for support. Her wool felt harsh under his fingers. Dimly he remembered that it had been so ever since it was soaked in the water of the grove spring. Then the thought drifted away.

Slowly, patiently, Star led him through the restless herd. He stumbled beside her, rubbing his streaming eyes. Dazed, he moved into the open and saw what she had brought him to see.

The jagged stones that had been heaped against the cliff face were gone, tumbled away as if by a giant hand. Now Rowan could see that the cliff and the slope were not separate but formed from one vast sheet of gleaming rock.

The stairway of his dream began where the rock started to rise steeply. He stared at it blankly through a haze of steam and tears. The stairway was shining, lit by a strange, yellow radiance that was not the sun.

He raised his eyes. Beside the stairway, from a great split in the rock about halfway up, flowed a river of gold.

The river of gold streamed slowly out of the rock.

Steaming, rich and thick as honey, it ran beside the stairway, down to the gentler slope where once the bukshah had milled and pawed the ground. And there it spread and moved on in a broad, gleaming golden band, to ooze over the edge of the drop.

I am dreaming, Rowan told himself. But he knew he was not.

The breaking heart will clear the way.

The heart of the Mountain had burst through its shell of rock, revealing its secret. And now the molten gold was running, running like blood down the slope and into the Pit of Unrin.

Rowan became aware that Zeel, Norris, and Shaaran were standing behind him, seeing what he was seeing. He could feel their presence. He could hear their rapid breathing. But none of them said a word.

He felt Star pull gently away from him, felt his hand fall to his side like a dead thing. He saw Star lumbering toward the stairway, over ground spattered with cooling splashes and puddles of gold, and the other bukshah following, one by one.

And as the beasts began to climb, Rowan's eyes cleared and he saw without surprise that they looked very much as they had looked in his dream, though far thinner and more wasted.

Their heads were held high. Their horns were

white and razor sharp. Their shaggy coats were thick and gleaming. Their hooves shone bright with gold, and where they trod they left golden prints behind them.

We must follow the beasts. . . .

Rowan moved toward the stair, and he also began to climb. He knew his companions were following, but he did not turn to look at them. He just moved up, one step at a time, while beside him liquid gold ran down, ran like steaming blood from the Mountain's heart, draining from the broken rock.

It was a dream that was not a dream. A dream of heat he could not feel. Of a plan he could not see. Of rags and wisps of memories his mind could not grasp. Of dread and suffering, yearning and regret, silence and death.

Only when he had passed the place where the golden river began did he look up. And there, not far below the patch of gray that marked the ice creepers' den, was the yawning mouth of his dream.

It was the entrance to a cavern, shadowed and ghastly, wreathed in billowing steam. A broad ledge of scarred rock jutted out below it, like a vast, deformed chin.

We climbed over it all unknowing, Rowan thought dimly. He looked from side to side, at the smooth, hard skin of the mountainside. *Beneath us* now beats the Mountain's heart, he thought. Its heat, smothered beneath the rocks, slowed the ice creepers and saved us. Saved us . . . for another purpose.

For this.

He turned his eyes upward again. He was nearly at the top of the stairway. Through the steam he saw that the mouth in the rock was not quite the same as the bare, gaping maw of his dream. Three tall, jagged stones remained stuck in its base, jutting upward like crooked black teeth.

For the first time since he had set foot on the stairs, Rowan shuddered in dread.

Four must make their sacrifice.

Rowan turned and looked behind him. Zeel met his eyes calmly. "So. We have arrived," she said.

Behind her, almost hidden by her broad shoulders, was Shaaran, breathless and wide eyed, the battered box of silks in her arms.

And behind Shaaran towered Norris, his face steadfast.

High above them, snow heaped the cliff top and the gray patch sealed the cliff face, protecting the freezing cold within. Ahead, steam billowed from golden shadow.

In the realm twixt fire and ice . . .

The bukshah were crowded on the pitted ledge. They were bellowing and pawing the ground.

Some were pushing at the rocks.

They want to enter the cavern, but they cannot, Rowan thought. The spaces between the teeth— the rocks—are too narrow.

He felt his heart lift a little. Whatever was ahead, the bukshah, at least, were to be spared it. Their task was over.

The companions reached the ledge and began to push their way through the bukshah. Again the beasts snuffled and nudged eagerly at Rowan, Zeel, and Norris but let Shaaran pass by with nothing but a glance.

"They do not like me," Shaaran said.

"They sense your fear of them," Rowan answered absentmindedly. Then he grimaced. If the smell of fear repelled the bukshah, why did they press so closely around him? His body was trembling with fear. His skin was prickling with it. He felt that terror must be radiating from him like heat.

He led the way to the opening. It was damp and gleaming. Steam drifted within it, faintly tinged with gold.

Star was in the center of the line of beasts trying to force an entrance. She had set her shoulder against the middle rock and was pushing, as she would push to flatten a fence. She had succeeded in moving it sideways a little. But thin as the bukshah were, the space created was still too narrow for them.

And never would she be able to push it inward. The cavern was a high step above the ledge. The rocks, all three of them, were jammed against the step.

"You cannot do it, Star," Rowan said quietly, putting his hand to her mane. "Save your strength."

Star raised her heavy head to look at him. Her eyes seemed filled with angry sadness.

"You and the herd have brought us here, and that is enough," Rowan told her, his throat tightening. "Now you must leave us to do . . . whatever must be done."

Star pawed the ground, made a deep, groaning sound, and again turned to push fruitlessly at the rock.

"No! Go back, Star!" Rowan urged, tugging at her wool, desperate to make her understand. "Take the herd back to the grove now, and wait. There is a little food in the grove, and there is water, and safety from the cold and the creepers. And perhaps . . . after a time . . . the snows will melt and you can return to the valley."

If we do what we must, he thought. If we have the strength to do what we must.

He rubbed his cheek against Star's mane, feeling its unfamiliar roughness against his skin. Then he pushed gently past her and slipped between the rocks.

The air was filled with shadowy golden mist. He could see little through the haze.

He raised his hand, found he could touch the roof with ease, and thought of the ice creepers coiling in their freezing nest not far above his head. Zeel, Shaaran, and Norris came through the rock barrier behind him, crowding him, and he moved forward.

The bukshah had begun to bellow again, Star loudest of all. The low cries echoed weirdly, echoed on and on, till the hazy air seemed thick with mournful sound.

"It is lighter ahead," Zeel whispered behind him.

Rowan looked and saw it was true. The cave entrance was well behind them now, but instead of becoming dimmer, the strange light was strengthening. They were walking toward a yellow glow that grew brighter with every step.

And the steam was growing less. It was only a thin veil now. The walls of the tunnel through which they moved were clearly visible. The roof hung low and glistening above their heads.

With a shock of recognition, Rowan saw cloaked figures walking not far ahead, walking in silence and in single file, walking in dread and despair while the faint bellows of the bukshah echoed dimly around them.

All is lost. . . . We are lost. . . . There is no escape. . . .

The figures shimmered and disappeared. Rowan felt his breath coming faster. The yellow glow was growing larger. Now he could see that where it began, the tunnel broadened, opening into a much larger space. He knew that there they would find the source of the light, the end of the journey.

His legs were trembling. With part of his mind—that part that was still his own—he longed to stop, to throw himself against the glossy tunnel walls, to cling to them, hold himself back. But it was too late for that. He was being drawn onward by something more powerful than himself.

Instead of slowing, he found himself moving faster. And suddenly dim golden light was all around him, and tremendous heat enfolded him, and he saw what he had come so far to see.

The roof of the cavern was low, and mottled black and gray. The black walls were veined with sparkling gold, lit, like the hazy air, by a radiance that streamed upward from a round hole in the center of the smooth, gold-veined floor.

There was nothing else. Nothing but heat, and shadows in the corners, and the echoes of the buk-shah mourning.

Like one in a trance, Rowan moved to the edge of the hole. Then he looked down—down into a pit so deep that his mind reeled. Down into the unimaginable heat, the terrible glare, of burning, molten gold.

Sick with dizziness, he gazed into the heart of the Mountain and could not look away. His head swam. He knew he had stopped breathing.

The hunger will not be denied,
The hunger must be satisfied.

"Come away, Rowan. Come away from the edge."

Rowan heard Shaaran's voice, but he could not understand the words. Other voices were claiming his attention. Voices from his memory.

Neel's voice:

We have offended the Mountain, and now the Mountain has turned against us.

Norris's voice:

If the people of the Valley of Gold had not died out . . . they could have told us how they made peace with the Mountain and ended the first Cold Time.

Zeel's voice:

That knowledge is lost . . . The Valley people did not share it . . . Perhaps they were too proud. Or ashamed . . .

"Ashamed," Rowan murmured. "Ashamed of what they had to do, to make amends. But our people will never know. Lann will not tell them, and I hope they will never guess."

The heart of the Mountain growled, waiting.

"And is this what must be done?" a steady voice asked. "If it is, I am ready."

22 ⌇ The Hunger

 Rowan turned. Zeel was standing beside him at the edge of the drop. She took his hand and met his gaze proudly. He saw her strength and grace, Zebak and Traveler combined, and his heart seemed to break within him.

"I am ready," she said again.

Norris stepped forward, and took Zeel's other hand. "I, too," he said. "I have followed you this far, Rowan, and if I must follow you down into the depths, and into eternity, I will."

Rowan looked at him, saw his courage and his open, honest face, and again his heart twisted in pain.

Only Shaaran had not moved forward. Only Shaaran had not spoken. But now she did speak, and when she did, her voice was trembling, but firm.

"I do not believe it," Shaaran said.

"Shaaran—" Norris began. But Shaaran shook her head.

"The Mountain is a thing of rock and earth," she said. "It is mysterious. It guards many wonders. But it requires only that we respect it. It does not want our love, or loyalty, or fear—or sacrifice. It does not need them. It needs—it must need—something else."

Rowan lifted his head as if waking from a dream. The medallion was throbbing at his throat. He turned. Shaaran was standing back from the drop. Tears were streaming down her cheeks.

One to weep . . .

"You are afraid, Shaaran," Zeel said softly.

"Of course I am afraid," Shaaran cried. "Anyone of sense would be afraid! But that is not why I refuse to join you in this madness. I refuse because you are wrong! Wrong!"

They stared at her blankly.

She stamped her foot. "Do you not have minds as well as hearts?" she demanded. "How can you think that throwing yourselves into the Mountain's boiling heart will cause one icicle to melt in Rin, or stop one ice creeper from being born, or make a single flower bloom?"

Rowan had turned around completely now. He took a step away from the pit.

A low growl came from deep below them. The rock trembled beneath their feet.

"We must not wait," Zeel urged faintly. "The anger is growing. There is too much heat. Too much—"

"Rowan, the medallion!" Shaaran urged. "Use it!"

"Each of us has asked a question," Rowan said. "We have had four answers. I fear . . . there will be no more."

But still he lifted his hand to the burning metal at his throat. It seemed to writhe under his fingers, as though it were alive. He felt words rising within him. He opened his dry lips and spoke. The words came easily, and he heard them without surprise, for they were very familiar.

"The beasts are wiser than we know
And where they lead, four souls must go.
One to weep and one to fight,
One to dream and one for flight.
Four must make their sacrifice.
In the realm twixt fire and ice
The hunger will not be denied,
The hunger must be satisfied.
And in that blast of fiery breath
The quest unites both life and death."

He stood quietly as the words died away. He felt very tired, but that was all.

"So . . . " Zeel murmured.

"Four must make their sacrifice," said Norris dully. "Here, in the realm between fire and ice. There can be no mistake."

But Rowan was listening again to a voice in his mind. Sheba's voice, saying the rhyme. He had just repeated it in exactly the same way. Every word, every pause. And . . .

"The line that ends in 'sacrifice,' and the line that ends in 'fire and ice' rhyme with each other, but there is a pause—a stop—between them," he said slowly. "They may be quite separate. I see it now, though I did not see it before. The line about sacrifice may be linked to the lines about the four souls that come before it. The line about fire and ice may be linked to the next lines, the lines about hunger. The rhyme reads quite differently then."

"Yes," Zeel said after a moment's thought. "But it does not really change anything. The four sacrifices still have to be made."

"Do they?" Rowan said. "Or have they been made already? Shaaran abandoned the silks to save me in the vale of horrors. Norris gave himself up as lost to save us from the ice creeper at the cave. You, Zeel, sacrificed your kite, and nearly your life, to save

Norris. And I—" He smiled wryly. "I sacrificed the most precious thing I had—your friendship and trust—to try to make you leave me and save your-selves."

"Yes." Shaaran nodded. "We all made sacrifices to reach this place. And now we are here. There is something we must do. Before—" She shuddered as the Mountain growled beneath their feet.

Before the rock bursts again, Rowan thought. Before the stairway falls, and the bukshah die. Before this cavern becomes our tomb.

"It is . . . about the hunger," Norris mumbled. "The hunger . . . "

The words hung heavy between them.

In the realm twixt fire and ice
The hunger cannot be denied,
The hunger must be satisfied.

Something flickered at the edge of Rowan's vision. He turned his head and saw movement in a shadowy corner just behind Shaaran. He saw the stirring of a bukshah-skin cloak on the floor, the feeble movement of a delicate hand as it curved protectively around a long wooden box. He saw another hand, a stronger hand, writing, and a bent head gleaming dark in the golden light. He felt the thoughts, the words scrawled upon the page. . . .

You must know how it was, when you return, and so I write these words . . .

And he saw the picture the mind was remembering. A picture painted on silk. A long line of people, trekking away over snow on a black, burned path. Ice creepers twisting from the mist of the Mountain. Bukshah standing together below, the only dark marks in an unbroken sweep of white.

The only dark marks . . .

The beasts are wiser than we know. . . .

Rowan drew a sharp breath. The moving hand stilled, a face looked up.

It was his own face. And in it he read the end of hope, the end of fear, the acceptance of what must be. The eyes stared at him blankly for a long moment, then the mouth seemed to curve in the shadow of a smile, and the head bent over the paper once more.

Rowan turned away quickly, his heart thudding in his chest, his mind grappling with the astounding idea that had come to him. He saw that his companions were looking at him in fascinated terror, their eyes filled with questions they feared to ask. He had always dreaded the day they would look at him like that. But it no longer seemed important.

"What did you see?" Norris blurted out, unable to

contain himself. "You were staring—at nothing! Was it our future? Was it, Rowan?"

Rowan did not answer. He did not even hear. He was listening to the echoes. To the echoes of bellowing that had never stopped—the calls of the starving bukshah, still milling at the cavern entrance.

The bukshah.

The bukshah, who had lived and died in the shadow of the Mountain for as long as the Travelers had wandered the land, and longer. The great, wise beasts the companions had saved from death in the grove. The beasts who had led them to this place. The beasts who had snuffled and nudged eagerly at him, and at Zeel and Norris, but ignored Shaaran. The beasts with their newly sharpened horns, their gilded hooves, their glossy coats hanging thick over thin, starved bodies . . .

Hunger . . .

Rowan looked around the cavern. Smooth black floor, veined with gold. Shadowed corners. Gold-veined black walls. Heat and light streaming upward from a well of fire to a low roof that was mottled black and gray.

Mottled gray . . . though the walls and floor were black.

He lifted his hand and touched the roof.

And in that blast of fiery breath . . .

Rowan whirled around and grasped Norris's arm. "Help me!" he gasped.

And he ran, with Norris, Zeel, and Shaaran pounding after him, their confused questions ringing in his ears.

Back through the mist they raced, the bellowing echoes growing louder, louder, white light taking the place of gold. Till there before them were the jagged rocks, the bukshah heaving vainly against them.

Star was still at the forefront of the herd. She raised her weary head.

"Back, Star! Back!" Rowan shouted.

Star saw him set his shoulder against the middle rock, with Norris beside him, and this time she obeyed. She backed away, and the other bukshah backed with her, till the path before the rock was clear.

Then Norris heaved, with all his great strength, and Rowan, Zeel, and Shaaran added their weight to his. And the great rock, loosened by the bukshah long before, rocked on its base, then slowly rolled away from the entrance.

The bukshah surged forward, Star at their head. The companions shrank back, flattening themselves against the side of the entrance. In frantic haste, the beasts pressed one by one through the gap in the rocks, half leaping up the shallow step into the tunnel and then breaking into a lumbering gallop.

The sound of their pounding hoofs was like thunder, the mist swirled like storm clouds. Rowan, Zeel, Norris, and Shaaran ran after them as they galloped toward the cavern.

"What are we doing?" roared Norris.

"We are doing what we should have done in the first place," Rowan roared back. "We are following the beasts. All along, our part has been only to make sure they reached the cavern. It is *they* who are needed there, not us!"

"Why?" Shaaran shrieked. "What are they going to do?"

But Rowan did not have to answer her, for as she spoke they reached the cavern, and she saw it for herself.

She saw the great beasts tossing their heads, and their newly sharpened horns, the horns of which she had always been so afraid, doing what they were made to do. She saw the horns sinking deep into the pale patches that dotted the cavern roof, digging out great chunks of thick, stringy gray. She saw the bukshah gulping down the gray chunks ravenously, as if they were the sweetest food on earth, then raising their heads to tear out more.

The hunger must be satisfied.

"This is the material the ice creepers use to seal their nest!" shouted Norris, staring panic-stricken at the crumbs of gray lying on the floor and the shower of larger pieces falling like enormous hail-stones from the roof. "The nest is directly above us—and the cavern roof is full of blocked holes! As full of holes as a sieve! Rowan, stop the beasts! They will dig straight through to the nest! They will be the death of us!"

"They will be our salvation," Rowan said.

But, sure as he was, even he held his breath as Star, with a mighty twist of her horns, ripped the last layer of gray from the huge hole above her head.

For an instant the hole was nothing but black rock encircling blue-white light. Then a hissing white horror was filling the gap from above, thrusting through it, needle-sharp teeth bared, blue throat gaping.

Shaaran screamed and screamed again. But the echo had not even begun when dark blue mist belched from the hissing mouth, the blue throat seemed to shrivel, and the ice creeper fell back, out of sight.

"It is the heat!" Rowan shouted over the noise of

the bukshah and the echoes. "The creepers cannot bear it! It is death to them!"

And he turned back to watch as one by one more holes were cleared and the heat of the Mountain's burning heart, no longer trapped within the cavern, gusted upward in a fiery blast to warm the hidden realms that the ice creepers had for so long, and with so much labor, made their own.

23 ∾ Life and Death

 In time the bukshah's frenzy slowed, and the process of digging out the strange food they knew would see them through the hardest winter settled into a steady, contented rhythm. Gray fragments littered the floor. Many holes were still blocked, but many others had been wholly or partly opened, and any ice creeper that had ventured near them had died in the hot air that gusted from below.

"So our quest has united life and death indeed," Norris said with satisfaction. "Death to the ice creepers, life to us."

"The ice creepers are not all dead," Zeel said, looking at him with amusement. "The great nest is destroyed, certainly, and the creepers who were marching downward, spreading the cold that was to their liking, are no more. But many others must still dwell in the high places of the Mountain, where the snow never melts."

She glanced up at the gaping holes in the cavern roof. "And as the heat continues to rise, and so grows less in here, they will be back, risking their lives to seal the holes again. It is in their nature to try to extend their territory."

The companions were sitting out of the way of the bukshah, against the entrance wall. Already it seemed cooler in the cavern, though they all knew by now that the heat was far greater than they could feel.

"I think the spring in the grove left a layer on our skin and clothes that protects us from the heat," Rowan said. "The bukshah's coats also."

"The passage to the vale of horrors sharpened their horns so that they would be ready to dig their food from the cavern roof." Shaaran shook her head in wonder. "And the water of the spring protected them from the heat that was to come. It is as though they were guided to follow the path they took."

"They *were* guided, I am sure of it," Rowan said. "Not by magic, but by ancient instinct. From the earliest days, the bukshah herd must have come to the cavern to feed in the winter. So every year the cavern roof was cleared, the ice creepers retreated, and the balance was kept."

"Then how did the first Cold Time come?" asked Norris. "Or was it just a legend after all?"

"Oh, no," said Rowan soberly. "It really happened, I am sure. I think that it happened because the people of the Valley of Gold decided to build fences, to keep the bukshah confined all year round."

"But why?" Zeel demanded. "Why would they do such a thing? They must have known what the bukshah did in the cavern! The Mountain was not forbidden to them, as it was to the Travelers."

Rowan sighed. "I suspect, though we can never be sure, that the people had discovered that the hotter the cavern became, and the more the pressure below increased, the more swiftly their secret river of gold flowed. They thought only of the beauty and power of the gold. They forgot that the Mountain had needs as well."

"And so the first Cold Time came," Zeel muttered. "The fools! At last they realized what they had done and corrected it. But they would not tell the Travelers how. No wonder! No wonder they were ashamed."

Rowan sighed. "I am ashamed also, for not seeing that there must have been a reason why the bukshah have always tried to stray in winter. The bukshah are wise, not stupid. I knew that, yet I did not try to understand them. Instead, like all the keepers of the bukshah before me, I coaxed them back to their field with the food kept to feed them through the cold months. Often I wondered how they had survived before we came to the valley. Now I know."

Zeel frowned. "But when the Valley of Gold was destroyed at last, the stairway, and this cavern, were buried in the landslide caused by the killer trees. The bukshah could not have come here to feed after that."

"No," said Rowan. "Through all those years they must have turned away disappointed and returned home with only the leaves from the grove to fill their bellies. Then we came to the valley, built fences as the people of the Valley of Gold had once done, and began to feed the beasts in winter. So though their instinct to go to the Mountain remained, the urgent need for food was not there, and they were content to keep away."

"And all the while, little by little, the creepers' seals were growing thicker in the cavern roof, and the Mountain was becoming colder," said Zeel. "And the creepers bred more and more, creating more cold, and the winters grew longer and more terrible year by year."

Despite the heat, Shaaran drew her cloak more closely around her.

"So if the people of Rin had not settled in the valley and begun feeding the bukshah in winter, the herd would have died out," said Norris.

"At last the whole land would have perished," said
Zeel. "As it is, the bukshah survived, to lead us here
and show us what had to be done." She glanced at
Rowan thoughtfully. "It was fortunate chance, it
seems, that your people came, with their fences and
crops and storehouses, and their ability to survive
the cold."

Rowan wondered. Fortunate chance? Or something else?

"Rowan, what did you see, just before you ran to
let the bukshah into the cavern?" Norris asked
abruptly. "You would not tell us before. Will you tell
us now? Did you see the future? Did you see—all
this?" He waved his hand at the feeding bukshah.

Rowan shook his head and slowly climbed to his
feet. He knew it was time. Time to solve the last
mystery. Time to share what he thought he knew.
He had been unable to speak of it while urgent
action was needed, and even after that he had kept
silence, hugging the precious secret to himself, as if
airing it might injure or destroy it.

If there is no proof, no trace, it will only be my
word, he thought. The word of a dreamer, easily
put aside and explained away. If there is nothing
left, how can I bear it?

But with his companions following closely behind

him, he began to thread his way through the buk-shah, making his way to the shadowy corner where he had seen the last vision.

The corner lay in darkness, keeping its secrets.

He stopped a little way from it and tried to light a torch, but his hands were trembling so much that he could not manage it. Glancing at him curiously, Zeel took the torch from him and lit it herself.

The flame flared up. They approached the corner.

And there, in a nest of dusty bones, lay a long, wooden box.

"Why, Shaaran!" exclaimed Norris. "You have left the silks . . ."

But his voice trailed off as he saw that Shaaran still clutched in her arms the box she had carried all the way from Rin.

Rowan knelt before the tangled bones and put his hands upon the box. The wood was iron hard, pre-served by the steady, dry heat of the cavern. The catch fell away from the lid as he opened it.

What he saw inside the box made his heart pound. It was a shallow tray holding a clutter of tiny glass jars, in every color of the rainbow. And lying on top of the jars, a scrap of parchment.

He lifted the parchment out. It was covered in weak, straggling writing. He read the words aloud.

My friends,

You must know how it was, when you return, and so I write these words. Fliss is too weak to do more.

Bron escaped the Zebak attack and ran back to warn us. He arrived in two days, despite his injuries. Following the plan, Bron, Fliss, and I took the treasure, left plentiful food for the horses, and followed the beasts on their secret way from the Valley of the Bukshah into Mountain Heart. Once we were safe here, we kept good watch. Every day we expected you to return, either driven by Zebak whips or blessedly free, but you did not come.

Rowan's voice faltered.

"What is this?" breathed Norris hoarsely. "I do not understand. Who—?"

"Be still, Norris!" Zeel hissed, her face intent.

Rowan swallowed the lump in his throat, and read on.

At the end of winter the bukshah left Mountain Heart, but we remained. From afar we saw the new crop bloom in our valley and sorrowed that we alone could see its beauty.

Again Rowan stopped. This was almost too much for him to bear. He could guess what that "new crop" was—sweet-smelling bushes loaded with fruit, bushes grown from berries brought down from the Mountain. The unknown writer had little realized what evil was disguised in that beauty. He had not known that from the pretty little bushes foul, flesh-eating trees would grow.

His companions were waiting, breathless. He forced himself to continue.

A little time afterward we saw that some dread illness had befallen the horses and the birds, for they lay still in the streets. Fearing a Zebak plot to tempt us out of hiding, we retreated into the cavern. A few nights later there was a fearful thundering. The ground shook, and when we arose, we found that the gate was dark and sealed by rock.

"They were in here when the killer trees erupted from the earth and caused the landslide," Zeel said grimly. "They were trapped." She looked down at the pathetic pile of bones, and her fists clenched.

Rowan took a deep breath, and read on.

Many weeks have passed since then. Bron has labored mightily to free us, but even his great strength cannot move the barrier. Our food and water are long gone. We are dying. But the treasure is safe, and we are together. This comforts us.

We grieve for you, our friends, but our hearts tell us that some day you will find a way to return, for the land will call

to you and you will hear. And when you return, you will
open Mountain Heart once more so that the bukshah can
enter as they must. Then you will find us, and lay us at last
in the good earth, beneath the open sky, where we long to be.

We leave with you our blessings.

Evan of the Bukshah

"Evan of the Bukshah," Zeel said softly. She had
tears in her eyes. The first tears that Rowan had
ever seen her shed.

He put down the parchment. Then he put his
hand back into the box and took out the tray that
held the tiny jars, laying it carefully aside. There
was a deep cavity beneath the tray. It was filled
with rolls of silk.

With a cry, Shaaran threw herself down and, with
trembling hands, reached into the box and took out
the roll that lay at the top. Tenderly she unrolled it.

Blue, white, and gray. A long line of people trekking across
white snow, following a burned black path . . .

"It is the same!" Norris whispered, his face filled
with fear. "It is the silk *you* painted, Shaaran."

"No," said Shaaran quietly. "It is far, far older than
that. See the faded colors? And . . . "

Her slender finger pointed to the bukshah standing
in the snow. "See, Norris? My painting showed the
bukshah fenced. But the people of the Valley of Gold

had torn down their fences long before this was painted, leaving the bukshah free to roam. The keeper of the silks—Fliss—painted only the truth, as we are bound to do. Ah . . . the work is beyond compare!"

And as Norris, Zeel, and Rowan watched in awe, Shaaran unrolled another silk, and another, and another. The silks were frail as gossamer, but the colors still lived, and the shapes still spoke.

The wise woman leading her people through the early snows to battle on the coast. The Zebak army attacking on the plains, fierce and unexpected. One injured man, eerily resembling Norris, escaping and staggering away. The same man, leaning on a long stick, telling the news to two figures in a valley paradise where paths were paved with gems, miniature horses wandered, and a golden owl with emerald eyes watched beside every door. Three figures, wearing furred cloaks, following a bukshah herd up steep stone steps toward the mouth of a great cavern . . .

"The people of the Valley of Gold *did* receive the Travelers' call for help," Zeel said in wonder. "They set out for the coast with the messengers, leaving only the keeper of the bukshah and the keeper of the silks behind. But on the journey they were attacked by the Zebak."

"They were captured, marched to the coast, loaded into ships, and taken away into slavery across the sea," Rowan murmured.

Zeel shook her head. "And the Maris and the Travelers were in hiding, and never knew. No one knew. Until now."

"But—" Norris's eyes were very wide. "But that means that—that—"

"It means that the people of the Valley of Gold were our ancestors," Shaaran whispered, unable to take her eyes from the silks. "It means that this land is not new to us at all. It is our place. It has been all along."

"A rich, varied people, big and small, strong and gentle, disappeared," said Zeel, trying to take it in. "Centuries later a band of tall, sober warrior slaves with no memory of their past arrived on the Maris shore. How could anyone think they were one and the same?"

"I think Ogden does," said Rowan. "Or suspects, at least. He knows more tales of the Valley of Gold than anyone alive. I would say that one of the things he knows is that history there was kept on painted strips of silk."

And as Zeel and Norris and Shaaran bent once more over the ancient treasures Shaaran was unrolling one by one, Rowan picked up the scrap of parchment and touched the scrawled words gently.

"We have returned, Evan of the Bukshah," he said softly. "We found a way. Just as you knew we would."

24 〰 Meetings

 And so it was that Rowan, Zeel, Shaaran, and Norris left the bukshah to their feast and came down from the Mountain, carrying far more than they had carried when they began their journey.

They carried two boxes of silks instead of one. They carried a knowledge that filled their hearts to bursting. And they carried the bones of the three who had perished in the cavern—Bron, the warrior, Fliss, the keeper of the silks, and Evan, keeper of the bukshah.

"They looked so like us, our ancestors?" Shaaran asked Rowan quietly, as they walked together.

"Very like," he said. "So like that I thought I was seeing our future. But we were only treading in their footsteps."

"And what of the shadow people? The starving ones you saw outside the cave? Were they . . . ?"

Rowan shivered under the sunlight. "I think they were far, far older," he said reluctantly. "I think they were some of our people who lived through the first Cold Time." Again he shivered. The memory of those familiar, tortured faces haunted him still.

Shaaran bit her lip, and for a long time they walked in silence. Then, at last, she spoke again. "Rowan, Sheba told you that only you could lead the quest. Have you thought why that was?"

Rowan nodded. "Because I am the keeper of the bukshah, and love and trust the beasts as they love and trust me. Because I am a dreamer, and the medallion would accept me. Because I have had . . . much practice in thinking of new ways to solve problems."

He swallowed. "And because—because you, Norris, and Zeel were my friends and would follow me," he added in a low voice. "For you were all needed, too, if the quest was to succeed."

Shaaran bowed her head. "I was wondering," she said, "if part of the reason Norris and I were called was that we were like the other two. The two long ago. Just as you were like Evan."

"Yes." Rowan hesitated. "And perhaps it was also because you and Norris represented the two halves of the people of Rin. And I . . . was the bridge between you."

"And I?" asked Zeel dryly, moving up beside them. "What was my part?"

"You stood for the Travelers, the Maris people, and perhaps the Zebak, too," said Rowan. "You were the witness."

The way was long, and full of hardship, but the companions were filled with happiness. For all around them the snow was melting and the land was awakening after the long, cold winter.

And as they reached the place where the water flowed down to Rin from the Mountain top, they came upon three figures kneeling to fill their flasks at the pool.

Jonn. Jiller. Allun.

Rowan stared at them in disbelief.

The three at the pool looked up, and their faces broke into smiles of pure joy. With a cry, Jiller flew into Rowan's arms. Allun and Jonn followed quickly, and soon the four companions were all part of a joyous circle.

"How can you be here?" Rowan exclaimed. "How could you know that it was safe to return?"

"We did not," said Allun cheerfully. "Quite the reverse. We thought we were tramping into the jaws of death, in fact."

"When Allun told us he had seen Zeel overhead,

speeding to Rin, we feared something new and very grave had happened," Jonn said. "We could not go on. We had to return."

"Marlie and Annad, too," Jiller said. "They are fretting back at the village, with Lann and Bronden. We came to try to find you—to help if we could. Though now it seems there is no need."

"Lann? Bronden?" asked Rowan eagerly. "Are they . . . ?"

"Both are well," Allun said. "Bronden is still very weak, but recovering—though when she finds out that Lann made bonfires with the village's whole supply of furniture, she may have a relapse. There is a busy time for her ahead."

Rowan glanced at Zeel. "Old, useless wood?" he murmured. Zeel shrugged. Tables and chairs meant nothing to her.

"And by the way, Rowan," Allun went on. "Sheba must have seen Zeel, too, and sensed that some of us would be returning to Rin. She came riding back along her black path, just before we left, to give us a message for you. She says to tell you that the medallion she gave you may look like base metal, but it is made of pure gold, and she expects it back the moment she returns. She says that you could not take her place in a thousand years, whatever you may think."

"I am glad to hear it," Rowan said with feeling.

"How can you waste time with nonsense about furniture and Sheba, Allun?" Jiller exclaimed. "The Cold Time is ending! We can see the proof all around us! Somehow these brave young ones have saved us all. But how? How?"

She turned to Rowan, her tearstained cheeks flushed with happiness and pride. "Tell us!" she begged. "What happened on the Mountain? What did you discover that has changed so much, so quickly? Where are the bukshah?"

Rowan's heart was too full to speak. And, in any case, he hardly knew where to begin.

"They will tell us all in their own time, no doubt," Jonn said calmly, putting his hand on Rowan's shoulder. "We already know the most important things. These four souls are safe. The long winter has ended. And the people can come home."

Rowan exchanged glances with Norris, Shaaran, and Zeel. He thought of all they had to tell. He thought of the sad, small bundle he carried, and of the place where he would bury it, with honor, under the great tree in Rin. He thought of the suffering, grief, mistakes, and waste of centuries.

Then he thought of the future, and he smiled.

"Yes," he said. "At last, the people truly can come home."

Read all the Rowan books!

ROWAN OF RIN
Pb 0-06-056071-1
A mysterious drought, an impassable mountain, a ferocious dragon—will Rowan and his companions live to save the day?

ROWAN AND THE TRAVELERS
Pb 0-06-056072-X
The people of Rin fall under a mysterious spell, and Rowan must travel to the evil Pit of Unrin to rescue them—if he can find the courage.

ROWAN AND THE KEEPER OF THE CRYSTAL
Pb 0-06-056073-8
To save his mother from a deadly poison, Rowan must face a venomous sea serpent. Can he defeat the vicious creature and find the antidote in time?

ROWAN AND THE ZEBAK
Pb 0-06-056074-6
When the Zebak, Rin's most ancient enemies, kidnap Rowan's sister, he dares a journey to their land to save her. If he fails, all of Rin could be lost.

AVON BOOKS *An Imprint of HarperCollinsPublishers*

Greenwillow Books
An Imprint of HarperCollinsPublishers

www.harperchildrens.com